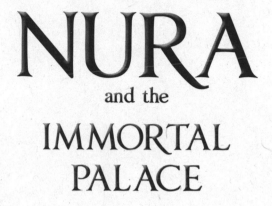

NURA

and the

IMMORTAL
PALACE

NURA

and the

IMMORTAL PALACE

M. T. KHAN

JIMMY PATTERSON BOOKS
LITTLE, BROWN AND COMPANY
New York Boston

JIMMY Patterson Books / Little, Brown and Company
Hachette Book Group
1290 Avenue of the Americas, New York, NY 10104
JimmyPatterson.org

First Edition: July 2022

JIMMY Patterson Books is an imprint of Little, Brown and Company, a division of Hachette Book Group, Inc. The Little, Brown name and logo are trademarks of Hachette Book Group, Inc. The JIMMY Patterson Books® name and logo are trademarks of JBP Business, LLC.

The publisher is not responsible for websites (or their content) that are not owned by the publisher.

Library of Congress Cataloging-in-Publication Data
Names: Khan, M. T. (Maeeda Tariq), author.
Title: Nura and the immortal palace / M.T. Khan.
Description: First edition. | New York : Little, Brown and Company, 2022. | Audience: Ages 8–12. | Summary: Searching for her buried friend after the mines collapse, twelve-year-old Pakistani mica miner Nura finds herself at the Sijj Palace, a luxury hotel for the dangerous and deceitful jinn, where she must discover the truth beneath the glitter or be trapped forever.
Identifiers: LCCN 2021040226 | ISBN 9780759557956 (hardcover) | ISBN 9780759557932 (ebook)
Subjects: LCSH: Jinn—Juvenile fiction. | Mica mines and mining—Juvenile fiction. | Mine accidents—Juvenile fiction. | Secrecy—Juvenile fiction. | Exploitation—Juvenile fiction. | Friendship—Juvenile fiction. | CYAC: Genies—Fiction. | Mines and mineral resources—Fiction. | Mine accidents—Fiction. | Secrets—Fiction. | Friendship—Fiction.
Classification: LCC PZ7.1.K5312 Nu 2022 | DDC [Fic]—dc23
LC record available at https://lccn.loc.gov/2021040226

ISBNs: 978-0-7595-5795-6 (hardcover), 978-0-7595-5793-2 (ebook), 978-0-316-46620-2 (international)

Printed in the United States of America

LSC-C

Printing 1, 2022

To my parents
for teaching me the value of education

CHAPTER 1

Sparkles in the Dirt

A lot of people dream of being buried by their money.

If these tunnels collapse, I might just get that wish, except none of the mica that's packed into the walls of this mine belongs to me. With my teeth gritted and two hands around a shovel, I strike the dirt wall in front of me. The earth splits apart and crumbles to the floor like an offering, flakes of mica glistening in a pool of orange sunlight.

I crouch, my trousers matted in dust, matching the grime that stains my body like a second layer of skin. I brush my fingers through the pile of dirt, sifting for the precious flakes and dropping them into a basket.

"It's not big enough. None of these are," I mumble. Where is the Demon's Tongue?

My stomach growls. I wonder if a tiger lives in there with how hungry I always get. As my thoughts fade into images of syrup-covered jalebi and juicy gulab jamun sweets, I leave the worthless pile and stumble deeper into the dark throat of the mines.

"W-wait, Nura! Don't go so deep," comes a whine from beside me. "It's d-dangerous—"

"I know," I grunt, cutting off Faisal's annoying warning for the third time today. "But Mr. Waleed sells gulab jamun on Tuesdays, and if I don't dig enough mica today to earn me the rupees to buy one, I'm going to blame you."

If anyone says that they work for passion or world peace and not the delicious food on their plate, they're lying. There's only one truth in this world: everyone's got a hungry monster in their stomach that roars if they don't satisfy it.

And I know well enough to satisfy mine.

It's why I'm searching for the Demon's Tongue, a legendary treasure buried deep in these mines. Maybe it's just a rumor invented by kids to spark some life into a boring job, but I swear I've heard even the contractors talk about it. It's money like no one has ever been able to grasp—it's magic, it's unearthly.... Maybe it can't even be seen. Maybe it's not even real.

I chase its myth as I creep forward. The tunnels are narrow—only fit for a kid's body. My baba used to work in these same mica mines, but when the tunnels tapered into thin paths as deep as three hundred meters, contractors learned that adults weren't the best people for the job. It's why a twelve-year-old like me and the other neighborhood kids got hired to dig up the mica scraps scattered underground.

The sharp clang of hammers against stone rams through my eardrums like the ticking of a clock, and the fading sunlight tells me I don't have much time left before we call it a day. I'm here from sunrise to sunset, from the moment my eyes crack open to the last second before my muscles scream at me to stop.

A sparkle flashes in the corner of my vision and I can almost taste the sweet gulab jamun on my tongue. My lungs protest—this deep underground, the air supply is low. I don't know much at all about science, but I can *feel* it, the chains around my chest that squeeze tighter as I lurch another meter below.

The mine is similar to a human. We enter through its mouth, dive down its throat, and then explore its dark belly. I fold my arms and duck my head into a slender tunnel. I'm just about to approach one of its arms.

"Nura," Faisal calls. "The sun's a-about to set. You w-won't be able to see anymore."

Faisal's always cautioning safety, but all the other kids and I threw safety into the sea when we accepted this job. The deeper the tunnels we dig, the greater the chance they'll collapse. And I've heard the horror stories too—about all the kids who never came back.

"Nura—" Faisal tries again.

"I'll be quick." If I don't reassure Faisal, he's going to talk my ears off. Giving warnings is one of the only times Faisal ever pipes up—his stutter is deeply ingrained and a constant source of mockery for the others. One kid is already glancing at him, but I'm not afraid to stomp my feet if they dare insult how Faisal talks.

"I can't let Ahmed beat me today," I say as I chase the glimmer of the mica shard. It's not the Demon's Tongue, but it has to be at least the size of my finger—a big catch that'll turn my haul into the largest one yet.

Sometimes if we dig up a promising collection of mica, the contractor pays us by the kilogram. It's a game for us, for all the kids who've never been to school or had the chance to glide on swings and play with dolls. If I can buy gulab jamun and beat Ahmed for the biggest haul today, then I'll risk it.

My bare feet slap against a muddy puddle as I hop down a ledge. I tuck my shovel under my armpit and crouch, just barely small enough to crawl through the tunnel and enter another cavity. Here, the mica is more stone than it is dirt, reserves not yet touched. The walls shimmer, streaked with green, white, and gold. It's like I'm sitting inside a jewel—a really hot and stuffy jewel. With torched air, my shirt clings to my skin. The heat is a smothering blanket.

"You found my favorite spot."

I crane my head to the side and see Aroofa, a scornful smile tugging at her lips. She flicks the end of her dupatta over her shoulder as she strikes a large stone against a smaller one, combing through the debris that bursts from the collision. Her younger sister Sadia is busy beside her, hammering clumsily away at the smaller rocks Aroofa throws toward her.

I sigh. Aroofa would be better and quicker with the hammer, but looking at the cuts and scrapes along her fingers, I know why she yielded the tool to her little sister. With so many people in the business, there's not enough equipment for everyone. You get here early and swipe a hammer or shovel, or settle for one of God's greatest gifts: your hands.

"Won't be yours for long," I reply, pointing to the kids that stumble inside the cavity, a smile creeping across my lips. Some of them are always following me, trying to copy my handiwork. When it comes to the largest hauls,

I'm second only to Ahmed, and he tends to disappear the second he hops down the mines. Me, on the other hand, I don't mind a little attention.

Aroofa's scowl deepens as the kids surround me, pretending to hack at the walls while their eyes stay glued in my direction. I roll my shoulders back. The stage is set. If they want a performance, I'm about to give those Bollywood actors a run for their money.

I narrow my eyes and catch the sparkle of the crystal. The shard is farther than I thought, a flash of white stuck in the folds of a crevice around a meter deep. I grunt as my arm reaches out. My cheek is squashed against the dirt, and the crowd of kids whisper to each other, curious about my overzealous efforts. I can almost feel Faisal's disapproval thicken the tension in the humid, grimy air, but I push forward, sliding my body into the narrow slot shaped like a crescent moon.

The light is fading. My vision goes blurry. Someone gasps behind me—I've scratched my shin against a rock. I can't even feel the trickle of blood down my ankle when the mica shard is so close—close enough that my fingers brush the smooth surface. One more grunt, and I dig my nails into the dirt around it, grasping the shard in my hand as I shout in glee.

"Got it! Out of the way," I yell as I pull backward.

The crowd behind me parts, their gazes locked on to my closed fist. I swat my shoulder-length hair out of my face as I stumble back into the mine's arm, up its throat, and leap toward the entrance of the tunnels. All around me heads are turning, and I can just make out Faisal's wide eyes as he joins the group chasing after me, shouting to show the treasure. But I want to see it shine.

As I climb out of the tunnel, my eyes narrow against the embrace of a bright sunset. Compared to the darkness of the mines, the surface is like a different world—one where golden rays wash over me and light the dirt on fire. Tiny, immeasurable shards of mica are littered across the ground, each one holding a flame.

I swallow gulps of fresh air, and it feels like my lungs grow three sizes bigger. The kids aboveground that are sifting through baskets of dirt glance over as I raise an arm to the sky and unravel my fingers—the mica in my hand shimmering against the amber sunset.

There's awe pouring from the surprised gasps. Some clap, others whistle. I lower the mica shard down to eye level, and light shines off it like a wink. It's the biggest piece anyone's found in weeks.

Most of the kids don't know why we dig these tunnels or

what mica is used for, but I've overheard plenty of conversations from the contractors to know why this streaky, colorless mineral has the world in a frenzy. It's used in paint and cosmetics—to make things sparkle.

I trudge toward my basket and drop the crystal into it.

I'm left with just the dirt.

CHAPTER 2

The Taste of Truth

Mr. Waleed's cart is an explosion of color. There's pink mithai, glistening brown gulab jamun, and bright orange laddu burning my eyes. My nose tickles at the heady scent, and I can almost hear the sweets chanting, *Buy me, buy me, Nura!*

Faisal clicks his tongue from beside me. "You're pretending the s-sweets are talking to you again, aren't you?"

We're standing at the edge of a dirt street in the town of Meerabagh, a few kilometers away from the mining site. I almost trip face-first into Mr. Waleed's cart as a motorbike zooms by, sweeping up clouds of dust. A goat bleats from the corner of the road, beady eyes staring at me, like it's laughing at my clumsy feet. The sky no longer bleeds reds and oranges, but deepens to a dark muted blue, beckoning the shops of the market to switch on their dizzying lights.

I love the market, even if it can't compare to what I've heard about the ones in Pakistan's big cities, like Lahore and Karachi. Shop lights flicker awake, flashing white, red, and orange—colors turned to their maximum brightness to capture as many buyers as possible. Handmade jewelry twinkles and jingles, a young man yelling the prices of the bracelets in the display case to anyone passing by. There are fruit stalls, clothing stores with racks upon racks of vivid, beaded fabric, and carts with toys that roll down the road in the hope that some kid will tug their parents toward it.

When night unfurls its fingers and rakes through Meerabagh, it makes sure to turn the usually quiet and dry streets of the daytime into a town that's alive with excitement. And I'm especially excited today—there's a few extra rupees in my pocket.

"Which one, beta?" Mr. Waleed asks me like I'm his own child. But the familial affection will stop once it's time to pay.

"You sure you don't want the laddu?" Faisal asks, eyes wide as he stares at the round orange balls. "It's like biting into happiness."

Mr. Waleed laughs at Faisal's ogling. Faisal should've

been a poet. He has the wistful gaze and delicate features of someone who's good with words. But none of us can really read. We've never spent a day in school.

I suck back the drool that threatens to spill down my lips. Eid al-Adha, one of the biggest Islamic holidays, is only a few days from now. It's the kind you spend with your family, remembering all that you're grateful for, and it's the reason sparks fly in my stomach this evening. Maybe if I buy something nice for my siblings, they might feel like we're actually celebrating. "Five gulabs, please."

Mining mica doesn't make you the world's richest kid, actually quite the opposite—we only do it because we're low on money. The daily pay is about two hundred rupees, which is barely enough to buy five pencils. But today—today I deserve something special, and I can't wait to see Maa's face light up at the sight of glistening gulab jamuns.

Faisal refuses to buy anything, even though I hear his stomach growl. Pink tints his ears, and I tousle his dark tangle of hair.

"No one in my family is as obsessed with sweets as you are. And my maa already made dinner," he whines in defense. "Are you sure you should even be buying th-that?"

My stomach sinks, and this time it isn't from hunger. "What do you mean?"

Faisal's gaze drops to the ground, his quiet voice barely

audible over car honks and shouting hagglers. "My family is saving up every rupee. I n-never get to buy anything."

My brows twist into a frown. It's like that for me too—Faisal doesn't have it any worse than I do. "I have three younger siblings," I snap back. "It's not like I can buy anything I want!" I point to the blue bicycle chained to the side of a stone shop. I jerk my head at a bright red dupatta that swirls around a girl's head. "I want that. And that. I'd buy the whole world if I could," I scoff. "What's wrong with a few gulabs?"

Faisal stares at me for a moment, brows creased, mouth set in a tight line. If he stares a second longer, I might punch him. But instead, he speaks. "You're going to keep on wanting things until you forget why you wanted them in the first place."

I still punch his arm.

I've known Faisal since we both started mining at six years old. He lives across the street from me, and his mother is a sweet angel with twin daughters she carries across her back like wings. Faisal's baba drives a truck from town to town to deliver crates of minerals and other loads. Sometimes I go to his house just to lie across the mud roof and drink in the sun, Faisal asleep next to me. He knows me better than anyone. Which means he knows exactly what I don't want to hear but will risk a punch to his arm to say it anyway.

We utter our goodbyes as the azan rings from the speakers, announcing Maghrib prayer and the day's descent into night. I turn a corner onto the next block, greeted with more stone shops and large paint-peeling white signs written in Urdu. I stop at a three-story building that looks like a sandcastle one breath away from collapsing. Cracks splinter up columns, and chunks of stone have fallen off the walls. I run a gentle finger across a hole in the surface, and pieces crackle to the floor.

I hate this. I wish Maa never had to work here. As I stride across the narrow hallway and poke my head into the door at its end, the room is cluttered with small tables of sewing machines. Women old and young are hunched over patches of clothing, trembling fingers aligning cloth against needle.

"Nura," my maa calls as she slips out the door, blocking my view of the room. "I told you to wait outside."

Maa's eyes are a watery brown, like diluted cane sugar, soft and unfocused from hours of straining them against dim light. She's always telling me to wait outside so I don't have to see the image of a hundred women with bright rolls of cloth in their hands, crouched so close together their shoulders almost touch, eyes flicking back and forth at every creak the building makes. But if I don't witness Maa working in this sweatshop, I'll forget why I mine mica.

Maa tightens the green dupatta across her head. She

counts the coins in her palm, tosses them into a small pouch, and slips it back into her shirt. Her bronze skin wrinkles as she takes a sniff, gaze sliding to me. "What's that smell?"

I pounce forward and raise the bag of gulabs. "Our favorite!"

Maa's eyes widen, and I snap on a grin.

But she doesn't mirror my excitement. "Nura."

I lower my arm, and the smile slips off my face. "What?"

Maa grabs my hand as she shakes her head. We trudge down the hallway and out of the creaky building, into the night air and under the flashes of yellow lights. I tug her arm, but Maa stays quiet, her dark brows furrowed. We step into the market, and Maa strides straight to Mr. Waleed's cart, where he slouches in a wicker chair.

Mr. Waleed's bony fingers pull the cigarette from his cracked lips as he puffs a cloud of smoke into the air. "Nasreen baji," he says to my mother, calling her *sister*, like they know each other past the occasional greeting.

Maa's lips are creased into a forced smile. "I want to return these." She lifts the bag of gulabs. A knot forms in my throat as Mr. Waleed flicks his half-lidded gaze between us, something like pity in his eyes when they land on me. But pity only lasts a few seconds in a town like Meerabagh— we're all trying to survive.

14

He bursts into laughter instead, waving her away as a customer lines up behind us. My cheeks are red hot like they've been slapped. I'm just relieved Faisal isn't here to witness the embarrassment. He would've clicked his tongue and shaken his head like a grandmother.

When Maa asks again, Mr. Waleed says, "Let your child enjoy something for once." It's enough for her to shut her mouth, grab my hand, and walk back to our hut at the outskirts of the town in silence.

CHAPTER 3

Stars Staring Down on Us

As Maa and I stumble back home, we pass hills shrouded in haze and towering rock formations. Our hut is a two-room rectangle slapped together with sun-dried mud, brick, and reeds. Wooden logs and thatch are strung side by side to form the roof. I smile at the newly painted scribble at the corner of the wall—that's definitely the mark of Kinza.

Before we even enter, my three younger siblings greet me at the door, hands flying to my neck as they tackle me in a fit of giggles. I want to play with them, but my stomach clenches in a strange twist, and Maa is still quiet as she hangs her coat on a hook and sits on the dirt ground next to the cloth that serves as our dinner table.

Adeel, the oldest of the bunch at eight years old, bites his lip as understanding washes over him. He's quick to pick up on things. When Maa and I are off working, it's Adeel who tidies our hut and makes sure my two younger sisters don't burn the place down. Speaking of those devils, Kinza and Rabia are still bumbling around, hopping toward Maa to plant a kiss on each of her cheeks.

"Nura, bring the gulab jamuns," Maa says.

I swallow nervously. I'm not even that hungry anymore, but I lurch forward and set the bag down. I sneak a glance at Maa, but there's no more fury in her eyes. The hard lines of her face have softened, brows tilted, and she looks at me like I'm a baby bird that tried to fly for the first time but instead flopped to the ground.

"Bacho," Maa calls to us—*children*. "Look at what Nura brought you."

My siblings rip the bag open, and gasps flutter from their mouths. I suppress a smile. *This* is what I wanted to see: the way their cheeks blush and the sparkle that swims in their eyes. We each take one sticky, syrupy gulab. I plop the round ball into my mouth and let it settle there, hoping my tongue soaks all the sweetness so that the flavor never washes away. Lightning jitters up my spine, and I can't help but release a noise of delight.

"Is it Eid already?" Kinza giggles as she licks her lips.

"Soon," I mumble, smiling at her through a mouthful. Eid is the one time our town goes out of its way to prove it's alive, and it's one of my favorite times of the year. Soon the streets will be brimming with families hopping door-to-door to share food. It's tradition to distribute meat among friends, neighbors, and the poor. When most of your town lives with empty pockets, it still doesn't add up to much—but I love it all the same.

Maa places yesterday's leftover dinner of rice and vegetable curry on a large plate, and we devour it like a flock of hungry vultures. There's still dirt in my hair, and Maa hasn't changed out of her sweaty shalwar kameez either, but we share a look of peace when we see my younger siblings absolutely delighted at the simple joy of food.

"Thank God for your dinner, and make dua for your baba," Maa says softly. We quiet down at that, whispering our gratitude to God and then praying our father makes his way safely to heaven.

Maa's eyes resemble wells now, glassy and on the brink of tears, but instead of letting them fall, she pulls my sisters into her lap and reaches to pat Adeel's bush of black hair.

Finally, she takes my hand in her worn, leathery ones, and I feel my breath strangle to release.

"Nura, I don't want you working in the mines anymore," Maa whispers.

She's been saying it more frequently these past few months, afraid I'm going to end up like Baba, who worked my same job years ago. But I don't have a choice. Faisal may call me stubborn, but I *did* get it from someone.

"Maa." I sigh. "We need the money." I could get it all at once—if I find the Demon's Tongue. But until then, I need to work every day.

My sisters are glancing at each other, still in the midst of learning the language to truly understand the weight of our words. Adeel only gazes down at the floor.

Maa's chest falls with a choked gasp. "I want you to go to school."

This is ridiculous. I know it. Maa knows it. I lost my will to go to school long ago. I knew I'd never have the money for education after Baba died. But I've accepted it. Who wants to sit in a boring classroom all day, anyway?

"I need to work so Adeel can go to school. Then Kinza and Rabia."

Maa shakes her head. Her lips are trembling now. I look away, and my hands ball into fists. I hate seeing her this way. "Are you saying this because I bought gulab jamuns? You just don't want me to have my own money, right?"

"Nura, *no*—"

I slam my fist against the floor. "Then let me work!"

Maa sighs and pulls me closer. She cups my cheek and settles my head across her shoulder, so that all four of her children are piled onto her like a blanket. My anger falls like the swoop of a summer bird, and a delicate breeze curls into my heart as Maa brushes her fingers through my hair.

"Let me tell you a story," she begins.

I can feel the anger in my stomach splinter into giddy butterflies. "Is it an excerpt from the Quran?" I ask, eager to learn more about the Islamic holy book.

"You and Baba's love story?" Kinza chirps. Adeel gasps in excitement.

"About jinn?" Rabia grins.

Adeel shivers and Kinza squeezes her eyes shut, both of them fearful of those invisible spirits born of fire and exceptional at trickery. I stifle a laugh. Sometimes I think Maa mentions them just so we do as she says. One time I lingered near the woods, and Maa pulled me back by the ear, saying jinn like to dwell in trees and would swoop down to capture me if I stayed any longer. Another time she caught Adeel skipping morning prayer and told him jinn were whispering the words of the devil in his ears. Do they work for the devil or for my maa? They might be helping her more.

"It is." Maa snickers as she tickles Rabia. "Your baba used to tell me this story all the time. He always tried to impress me."

"Tell us!" Kinza whines.

Maa hums, her gaze skyward, glancing at the glittering stars that hang above the streets of shimmering dirt. "Baba was walking down the road one night, when he stopped under a tree to drink his chai. He kept on hearing voices and a teasing laugh. But there wasn't anyone around him, and the road was empty."

Adeel squeezes Maa tighter, mumbling a quiet prayer.

"But then he looked up. He almost dropped his chai. Sitting on the branch above Baba was a man who looked just like him."

Rabia bites her nails.

"The man who looked like Baba had just enough differences that they didn't look identical—his brows were bushier, his nails were pointed . . . and that's when your baba knew that he was looking at his own qareen."

"Qareen?" I mutter. I've never heard the term before, not even from Faisal's superstitious father.

"Yes," Maa says. "A qareen is a type of jinn. It means 'constant companion.' Like your own shadow. God bestows everyone in the world with a qareen—and that night, Baba saw his own. The qareen tried to trick your baba into going in the wrong direction, tried to give him suspicious things, and kept following your baba even when the paved road turned to dirt."

I suck in a breath. Jinn are born tricksters. Everyone knows that—it doesn't take an education to be warned of them. The wizened grandmothers around town gather kids and tell them stories about how jinn haunted their homes, misplaced items, or tried controlling their bodies. You don't go near an abandoned site if you've heard rumors about jinn sightings or felt the air shift. They aren't fairy tales. It's kala jadu—black magic. My uncle once met a jinn, and he stopped going out at night ever since.

"What did Baba do?" Kinza mumbles, eyes still shut.

"Your baba recited Ayat al-Kursi." Maa smiled. "It's the throne verse in the Quran. God will always protect you from harm if you recite it. The jinn disappeared after that."

I fidget with the hem of my shirt, picking at a dirt stain. "But if reciting the verse keeps you out of harm . . . why isn't Baba here with us now?"

Maa smiles and pulls me close, and behind all the sweat and dust, I smell cinnamon and cumin powder, love and comfort, and peace. "Baba is looking out for us from above. Whenever you think of doing a bad thing, remember that Baba is always watching."

"So if I'm taking a dump, is Baba watching that too?" Adeel snickers.

Maa slaps the back of his head. I burst into the longest laugh I've let out in a while.

"Nura," Maa whispers to me. "Tomorrow is your last day working in those mines. No arguing with me."

I freeze. I don't want to act up in front of my siblings—they don't need to listen to our money problems. And the tone that Maa uses with me is the kind a general would use to command an army. She doesn't even want to hear a grunt of disagreement leave my mouth.

Tomorrow, I face the mines again. As a kid, I'm not supposed to be working. It's illegal across almost the entire world. But when I come home to Maa's soothing words and the hooligans that are my siblings, I could mine mica for the rest of my life if it meant preserving this little bit of happiness.

Yet that's what Maa is scared of. Me mining mica for eternity until I fall to the same fate as Baba. But if I stop working, Maa's going to have to pick up extra shifts, maybe even work a second job. I know she doesn't want to lose me, but what if I lose *her*?

Maybe there is a solution.

Tomorrow will be the last day I mine mica—because it's going to be the day I find the Demon's Tongue.

CHAPTER 4

Dig a Little Deeper

My feet are as light and quick as a burst of wind. I'm skipping over the hills near the edge of town, gold streaking the sky as the sun rises.

I like taking this particular route to the mines—it's not the fastest, nor the easiest to maneuver around, but it reminds me of my baba. He used to leave our hut as the blushing light of dawn trickled in, and I would sneak out after him to see where he would go. I used to think I was slick—hiding behind rocks and keeping as silent as a snake, but Baba definitely knew I was tailing him....It was the reason he chose to travel the route I'm currently on, so I wouldn't be able to follow him and find out where he was working: in the same mica mines I do now.

I was seven when my baba died. All I remember is his back—hunched from striking dirt, arms worn thin, and matted black hair as messy as my own. I wish I remembered something nicer about him. Maa always says she fell in love with his smile.

I sigh as I kick a rock out of my path. It tumbles down the hill, onto a gravel road, and under a leather shoe as it goes *crunch*.

My head snaps in the direction of the sound. Children skip across the gravel road, white shalwar kameez suits fluttering in the breeze—the uniform of Meerabagh's southern elementary school. Bags slung over their shoulders, they giggle and shove each other before heading past the school gate.

I stumble down the hill to stroll across the dirt path next to it, my gut clenched. It's a flat one-story building, designed with cream-colored concrete and red accents. There's a field of straw-like grass, kids kicking a soccer ball back and forth as they wait for the school bell to ring.

My stomach turns. I flick my gaze away. I'm not jealous or sad that I can't go to school—in Meerabagh it's only ever been about surviving. Bumbling old grandpas are rare in our town. . . . Most people don't live past sixty.

"Hey! Could you pass me that?"

I walk a few more paces before the voice yells again, a hand waving to the left of me. I turn and realize one of the schoolgirls a few meters away is pointing to a wooden pencil at my foot.

I lower my hand—my scratched-up, dirt-stained hand—and pick up the foreign object. I don't think I've ever held a pencil before. The ridges feel awkward in my fingers, and the point is dull as if the schoolgirl has used it too many times to count.

"It's not like you need it anyway," she calls.

My hand twitches, and I swallow a lump in my throat. I guess my tattered rubber sandals and grimy trousers that never look clean no matter how many times I wash them gave away my identity. It's not a secret that a lot of kids, especially at this end of town, are mica miners.

I look at the schoolgirl, probably the same age as me, and meet her waiting gaze. She has two more pencils stuffed into her pocket, but she still stretches out a hand in my direction. I raise my brows at the stick of wood. *Does this thing hold that much power?*

I scoff and toss the pencil to the schoolgirl. *Nah.* If there was something I wish I could have in my hands right now, it would be a gulab. Education, learning…don't make me laugh. I'll save that kind of boring stuff for my younger siblings. Mining mica is more exciting anyway.

❖

"Hand me that shovel."

Faisal tosses me the tool, and I barely turn my head to grab it. It's still morning, the daylight a pale wash of yellow as it strikes through the entrance of the mines and singes the top of my dark hair. The day's work has only just started, but grunts already escape my throat and sweat rolls down my neck in a plea to slow down. If my body can tell me that much, Faisal yaps even more.

"What are y-you in such a h-hurry for?" Faisal mutters. He strikes the dirt wall ahead of him with a pickaxe and winces when his finger gets cut on a pointy stone. I scoff. Faisal can be content with his bare minimum accomplishments, but I didn't jump into these tunnels for another day of mindless mining. Today I scour these passages for something *more*, something bigger, something magical, even—the Demon's Tongue.

"I want to get my family something nice to eat for Eid," I say instead. Not exactly a lie, but not a clear confession either. "I need to work twice as hard to get some extra cash."

"It's because Nura doesn't want to lose to me," Ahmed pipes up, a smirk snapping onto his face. He drops another shard of mica into his basket, chuckling when my gaze lingers on the large collection he's already amassed. He's all scrawny bones with a tight layer of skin strapped over—but then again, we all are. And it's the way I see myself in his image that irks me; Ahmed is also the oldest child, he lives with his single father and has five younger siblings, and yet he's able to help them live better than me with my own family. He wins our game *every single day*.

I grin. Except yesterday. Yesterday I tasted the sweet victory of being number one. Today, I'll turn the tables irreversibly. "I won't lose. Never again," I say.

Ahmed watches me with an amused smile. His answer comes in the form of his fingers dropping another flake of mica into his basket.

Darn it. I trudge forward and smack my shovel against the wall. The dirt falls like a rain shower, and I drop to my knees to sift for mica flakes.

Faisal scoots closer to me, his stutter a whisper. "D-don't let Ahmed get to you. Being greedy never does any good."

I glance up to see his wide eyes and tilted brows, lips stuck in a small pout. I almost want to smack him with how mature he's pretending to sound. "Did you hear that from your baba? Last time I came over, he also said his itchy palms meant money was going to come his way. And instead, you spilled the bucket of drinking water he brought only an hour ago."

Even in the dim light, I can see the red that flushes Faisal's cheeks. I reach up to tug at his curls like a grandmother would, but Faisal swats my hand away, already too embarrassed.

"Just take it easy," he murmurs. "You cut your leg yesterday."

I barely remember, and I can barely even feel it. It's just a red line down the side of my shin. Nothing unstoppable. Faisal might be satisfied with a few baskets of mica, or the wheezing boy next to me might pat himself on the back for going a day without stubbing his toe, but I wouldn't be able to call myself the best mica miner in all of Meerabagh if I *took it easy.*

I laugh, leaning into him to finally whisper my secret. "Not today I won't. I'm going to find the Demon's Tongue."

Faisal stumbles back and drops his basket, a cloud of dust erupting. His eyes widen to the point that I think they're going to escape his sockets. "T-the Demon's Tongue?" he whispers harshly, eyebrows raised.

I nod, my lips curling into a smug smile. Now that the declaration is out in the open, I feel even more determined to find it.

"Y-you know it might not—"

"It's real," I say with a straight face. Faisal can't refute the resolve in my gaze.

He gulps. "All anybody knows is that it's a treasure to take you from rags to riches. But you don't know what it looks like, tastes like, smells like..."

Legends of the Demon's Tongue began during my baba's time working in the mines, and since then, it's only gained more ground. "A treasure like that you can only know once you've seen it," I point out. A glimmering crystal, a chest full of gold—the description isn't necessary, only finding it is.

He bites his lip, about to hurl another warning, but I won't hear it today. Not when Maa practically begged me to stop mining. And my gut tells me it's not just for my family, it's for me too. I *want* to find it. I want to be the one that uncovers the myth and sinks into its magic.

"Don't worry, Faisal, I'll share some of my treasure with you." I laugh.

My hands get to work. It *has* to be here. People have been digging these tunnels for a decade. The mines probably sprawl over hundreds of meters. If the Demon's Tongue is really hiding within this sparkling dirt, it could be found any second, with any chip in the wall. And that's what I do—I hack away at the dirt, digging in the very deepest tunnels, seeking uncharted territory. Some kids send confused glances my way, others with raised brows and cocked heads. Someone calls out, "Be careful!"

I can barely hear anything outside my own panting and grunts, the air around my head fuzzy with dirt and suffocating breaths.

Closer.

It's a hiss, and at first, I think a snake has wrapped itself around my foot. But I strike my shovel farther, and I hear it again—a raspy whisper like the grating of stone against stone.

Come closer.

The hairs on my skin stand up. My lungs feel clogged, and my tongue is dry sandpaper, but that whisper plays in my head like an enchanting song. I can't help it when a smile twists onto my face and my arms work faster, slashing at the dirt to hear it again. I should be scared. I should wonder whether the heat has pulled me into a dizzying state, and I should've heeded Faisal's warning to take it easy. But all I can think about is the Demon's Tongue. I can almost taste it—and my stomach growls in agreement.

Legends say the miner who first got hold of the Demon's Tongue tried to keep it hidden, but within a few minutes, others were fighting underground for a chance to snatch it. The squabble brought the mines to a collapse—and that treasure, unlike anything ever seen before, was buried with it. Some claim the treasure moves around, slinking between the labyrinth of the tunnels. Others believe it's planted too deep into the earth for any human to reach.

Something sparkles a few meters in front of me. But it's not the streaky shimmer of a mica shard like the kind I saw yesterday. Whatever it is, it glows like molten metal just out of the furnace. Is this... Could it be?

Closer.

A grunt escapes my throat as I outstretch my shovel and strike whatever's glowing. Its light shuts off like a switch. What happened?

"Nura!" It's Faisal's voice this time, trembling and loud as it echoes through the tunnels and reaches me. But my mind is hazy, and my arms are moving on their own, so I ignore Faisal's protest. He does this every day. "You're digging too deep. S-stop!"

I hear the rumbling before I understand.

The ground shakes beneath me, and crackles of dirt overhead scatter into my hair. I hear kids yelling and the slapping of feet as they dash toward the entrance. I can barely see the entrance's pocket of light in the depth of the tunnel I've dug, and Faisal notices this as he runs toward me.

His brows are threaded with dread, forehead sweaty as he calls out to me again.

I don't know how I got so deep. My arms feel like limp strands of rope, all energy wiped from them. It's as if the efforts of my mining have caught up to me all at once, and panic pulses through my veins. There's an alarm in my head, and it's ringing loudly, telling me to move my feet, but I'm *stuck*.

I don't have the energy to move.

The rumbles get louder, as if an engine roars in my ears. The walls are trembling, about to cave in, and I taste the tang of metal and terror in the air.

"Nura," Faisal gasps. He lunges toward me and grabs my sagging arm, pulling me toward the entrance. I manage to stumble to my feet and thrust forward, hoping to catch a glimpse of sunlight.

All I hear is the dark and low roar of the earth splitting apart and the yells of the kids around me. But when I take another step, a whine pierces my ears. The grip on my arm vanishes. I snap my head around. Faisal's on the floor, half buried by a pile of dirt and stone.

This can't be happening.

His arm reaches out to me, fingers desperately out-stretched. I scream his name and pounce toward him, but a hand wrestles my wrist backward. "Nura," Ahmed shouts. "Get out now!"

"No!" I yell. I squirm in his grasp and shove him away, but Ahmed yanks my arm toward the entrance, and with it, all the energy left in my body. But Faisal still calls for me, I can hear it in my ears, or maybe that's not him, maybe this is all a bad dream, and it's that raspy whisper playing tricks in my mind. Perhaps I'm so hungry I'm hallucinating, I'm so tired that I can't comprehend the screams around me and the darkness that swallows my surroundings as everything goes black.

CHAPTER 5

Nothing at All, Only a Name

S tay back."

The few contractors who rushed over to the mining site have their hands on their hips and sweat on their brows. They share glances from the collapsed mining tunnels to the huddle of trembling kids.

It's late afternoon, and usually the sun rays punish our backs like whips of heat, but today the sun hides behind a shroud of dark clouds as if it's as scared as I am to learn the outcome. I sit next to Ahmed, our usual game forgotten, baskets left in the tunnels. We don't even try to find comfort in each other's gazes. Even though I don't mutter a word, I'm sure he smells the agony that seeps out of my skin like sweat.

I can't tell how long it's been since the dirt tunnels caved in. Once the contractors found out, they sprinted over and sprang down the mines. We've been waiting for two of them to pull out the kids who got trapped underneath. To pull out Faisal.

My lungs ache, my legs are trembling, and all the veins in my body have twisted into a knot.

"Let me take a head count again," one contractor says.

He points at us as his mouth runs through numbers. "Thirty-five, thirty-six...thirty-seven." Dragging a hand down his face, he turns to the other contractor next to him. "Five of them are missing."

I swallow. *Missing.* They'll be found. I know it. We just have to wait a little longer.

Just then, my prayers are answered. Someone shouts from within the darkness of the mines, and the contractors rush toward the entrance. I follow them, my feet moving before my mind even second-guesses. I stand at the edge, eyes narrowing as I notice something shift in the dim light.

"Help him up!" It's a contractor. He's holding a boy, outstretching his arms toward the men on the surface. Another contractor drops to his knees and pulls him out.

My heart's beating so fast I think it might grow wings and fly away. Dirt covers every inch of the boy, obscuring his eyes and clogging his windpipe so he's wheezing. I scurry over to the contractor to get a better look.

It's not Faisal.

I suppress the sound of worry that grumbles in my throat. There could be others. The contractor is still down there—

"He's the only kid I found."

My heart stops beating altogether. "What do you mean he's the only one?"

The contractor shakes his head, waving his arms for the crowd of kids to back away. "The others are gone."

I don't believe it. I can't accept it. Five of them trapped, and only one was saved? No. No. *No.*

After that long, dreadful wait, all the contractors can say is "Don't come tomorrow."

"But why did the tunnels collapse?" one girl sniffles.

A contractor shakes his head. "It could've been any kind of misstep. Maybe someone struck a loose wall or dug too deep."

I swallow. I don't want to think about it. It could've been anyone, or any*thing*. Maybe fate is playing a game. Maa likes to say destiny has already shaped our lives for us. I huff out a strained breath. Maa warned me of this. She warned me that I could fall to the same fate as my father. But instead, destiny chose Faisal.

I can't stand it.

The other children get shakily to their feet, rubbing tears from their eyes as they scramble home. I stay still. Ahmed sends me a questioning look, but he knows better than to ask. The contractors tell me one more time to get home before jumping into their cars and leaving too. As the sun dips below the horizon and creaky lamps light the mining site with a flickering yellow glow, I'm the only one left.

I grab my shovel.

This time I don't do it for the Demon's Tongue. I do it for Faisal.

Darkness embraces me as I hop into the mines. I keep a flashlight in the belt loop of my trousers, and the spot of light bounces every time I take a step. I hear pitter-patter, and at first, I think someone's walking around these tunnels as well, but when a droplet of water splashes against my forehead, I sigh. It's raining.

I can't tell if it's because of the weather, but the farther I hack into the piles of collapsed dirt, the more humid it gets. I don't let it curb my focus. All I can think about is finding Faisal. And hoping he's still alive. He has to be. Who's going to laugh at his baba's bad jokes?

It's endless. These mines go on forever. They'll swallow me whole. My arms are shaking from the effort. I don't know how long it's been, but now the dirt is wet and sticks to my feet, squishing with each step I take.

Three more strikes. I'll go back home if I can't find him in three more strikes.

Faisal's first day as a mica miner trickles into my mind. The way his thin limbs looked so fragile, I thought he'd snap in two just by lifting a shovel. When I asked him a question, only for him to shake his head, refusing to speak. I learned the reason a week later, when some kids shoved him around for stuttering in every sentence.

I strike the dirt and it falls away, but only more soil is ahead. I keep at it, grunting as my arms beg me to stop. *One.*

I remember the first time Faisal invited me over to his hut, and how my image of him completely transformed. At home, he helped his maa cook dinner, his baba clapped him on the back proudly when he learned a new word, and his twin sisters always begged him to play tag with them.

Two.

And then there's the day we lay across the rooftop of his hut, the sunset painting our faces in a golden glow, as if for the first time magic had weaved into our lives. The day my heart almost stopped when he said the most ridiculous thing to me.

My heart strangles the same way it did back then, but this time, out of guilt. Is it my fault that Faisal is gone? Did I take him away from his family? I have to find him.

Three.

The dirt wall ahead of me falls apart. Faisal isn't there. But something else is.

I lurch forward, and my foot dips into water. There's a puddle, and it's getting bigger as more water leaks from the wall behind it. Did I hit some kind of pipeline?

I smack my shovel against it, and the dirt crumbles away, making a hole big enough for my body. I gasp.

Outside the hole, the sea welcomes me.

It's not just any sea; it glitters a dazzling shade of deep pink. When I stick my head out to get a better look, my foot slips on sludge, and I plummet straight into the pink water.

"Gah!" I yelp, flailing to the surface. Even though I don't know how to swim, the water doesn't let me drown. Somehow it feels like a swarm of arms is keeping me afloat. I rub the pink water out of my eyes and look up at the sky—it's violet, with red clouds and shimmering yellow stars.

Where on earth am I?

I snap my head in all directions. Behind me, I see a small cliff and the hole I dropped out of. Around me, only the pink sea. But when I squint and stare ahead, I catch a glimpse of bright lights—blue, yellow, red—in the distance.

The waves carry me toward them. I think about Maa, about getting home before she starts worrying, but I don't have the energy to try to swim against the current.

Could the Demon's Tongue be here?

Maybe I've lost my mind. Maybe all that dirt and mica coating my brain has finally burst my bubble of sanity. But maybe—in this weird world of purple skies and pink seas...I can find Faisal.

CHAPTER 6

The Shadow That's Always with Me

I don't know how long I've been swimming, but the lights in the distance seem to glow brighter. I'm not entirely alone either. When I finally get a better look at my surroundings, I wonder if I hit my head somewhere in the mines. The sea isn't just pink—it shimmers a different color with every blink, as if a rainbow layer of oil swirls over it. And when I peer closer, odd shapes are swimming next to me. There's a fish that's as round as a soccer ball, with a pattern of stars across its scales. I gasp as a giant whalelike creature emerges from the sea some meters away, its mouth gaping in a yawn as bubbles fly out and burst into a shower of gold sparkles.

Where am I?

This can't just be my lack of education, right? These are creatures that look like children's drawings, painted with the brightest colors and a messy scrawl. I can't stop staring. But I also can't help the twist in my gut that's telling me I'm in danger. I lift an arm to shield myself against the splash of seawater as the whale dunks back down, but some flecks still land in my mouth. I raise a brow. The water isn't salty. It's *spicy*.

As I'm wondering if I should bottle some of this seawater and bring it back to Maa for curry, a few slender boats sneak into my vision, heading in the same direction as me. Red lanterns sway with each row of the boat, casting the sailors in an ominous glow. Finally, other people!

"Hey!" I yell as loud as I can, but it's easier said than done when half of my body is flailing underwater.

One of the boats notices me, and the rower makes a smooth maneuver to sail in my direction. I wave my hand excitedly, but as the boat gets closer, my hand stops waving, and then it drops.

Those aren't people.

Red fangs, tall pointed horns, fur like a lion's mane, skin

in varying bright colors—I can't breathe when I catch sight of what I'm looking at. They're twisted creatures, fashioned in an almost hideous form, something I'd only see in my worst nightmares.

"Care for a ride?" one snarls wickedly. He's got three eyes at the center of his forehead and a pair of yellowing fangs that hang over his bottom lip and reach his chin.

I try to swim away. My heart pounds against my chest like a warning.

But their hands reach out and dip into the water. One of the creatures has an abnormally long arm that unfolds like a ladder, and it nearly picks me up by my hair before I duck underwater. They burst into a fit of raspy laughter.

Another bright boat approaches me from behind, but it's a type of miniature cruise ship, with strings of lights cascading across it and hanging over its railings. The patrons on the ship peer at me questioningly, and my lungs constrict when I realize they're the same race of strange creatures. They heckle, throwing their drinks up in the air as if to salute my demise.

"What's a weak human like you doing here?" a creature with green skin and curling yellow hair asks. She's wearing one of the most elaborate shalwar kameez suits I've ever seen.

I can't believe I even considered wandering this place. It's clear that this *isn't* a place for humans, but frankly, I didn't know there was a place where humans *aren't* allowed.

My gut twists. I'm surrounded now.

The creature with the large fangs snaps his fingers, and a small flame appears in his hand. I gasp. Fire doesn't just come out of thin air, right? Maybe this is when school is supposed to come in handy.

"Lost children get torched." He snickers, then he throws the fireball my way.

I yelp before ducking underwater again, the flames quenching before they reach me. I bob my head upward, but he sends another fireball, and this time it manages to burn a lick of my hair before I dodge. I wonder if I'm hallucinating, or if God is punishing me with the worst nightmare of my life. More of the creatures join in, throwing objects or singeing my hair with rays of fire.

"Stop!" I shout, but my voice is buried by their laughter.

"So you're finally here?" comes a voice on the small cruise ship. The heckling creatures part as someone who looks just like me strolls to the edge of the railing.

She has blue skin, and her short hair is more jagged than mine, her nails angled in dangerous peaks—but that's *me*. Same eyes, same smile, identical lazy slouch.

"Y-you're my..." I don't want to say it. This can't be real.

"Qareen?" she answers for me. I can't believe it's the constant companion Maa warned me about.

And then it hits me. These aren't just any kind of nightmarish creatures. These are jinn—born of fire and living for trickery.

My qareen waves her arms, and her bright orange shalwar shimmers under the cruise lights. "Move aside, everyone. I invited her." Red eyes glinting, she reaches down and extends her hand to me.

My stomach churns, and I feel my insides fight to burst from my mouth. As my qareen stretches a hand toward me, I hesitate to hold it. All the warnings Maa hammered into me echo through my mind. *Jinn are tricksters. They're selfish. They can't be trusted.*

I yelp as another fireball lands right next to me. The intense heat floods over my skin like a hot shower. I have to get out of these waters—the other jinn may eat me alive. My hand twitches, but I clasp my qareen's palm, and she pulls me on board the cruise ship.

The jinn who found joy in torturing me now look away, bored, as if I'm just another speck of dirt. Fine by me. I try to run a hand over my chest to soothe my galloping heart, but my qareen doesn't let go. She's still smirking at me, red eyes twinkling, nails scraping the inside of my palm.

I swallow, but I don't look away. I won't back down. She's technically a part of me—like a shadow. Except she was a shadow in my world, and I have a sneaking suspicion that we're no longer in my world but in *hers*, and those rules don't apply here.

"Where are all these boats going?" I ask.

She points to the bright lights I saw in the distance, but now I can see an outline of a large structure with curved, arched roofs. "You've been invited to the Sijj Palace," she rasps, in a lower tone than my own. "Welcome to the realm of jinn."

CHAPTER 7

Look Below the Surface

The cruise ship's horn blares as it docks on the shore of an island with green sand. The docks are busier than Meerabagh's market—runners unload cargo from ships, dog-looking jinn with full faces of fur bark orders back and forth, and jinn wearing yellow peacoats usher the patrons on the boat toward a stone path. Is this a resort?

I've only seen something so luxurious on TV. On some occasions, the contractors would order a few of us to come by their office and package the mica for a bit of overtime cash. While our hands were busy, our eyes would be glued to the staticky box with its bright screen and crackling sound. One time a contractor left it on some vacation channel, and I'd never seen places so magical. I could never even *dream* about such possibilities.

My mind snaps back to reality as every color, light, and loud noise tramples over me. I have no choice but to follow my qareen if I don't want to end up as a toy for jinn again. I stumble down onto the wooden dock, and a sudden bout of dizziness almost knocks me off my feet. The purple sky is a deep violet now, indicating the descent into night, but it seems the jinn festivities are only beginning. Mosaic lanterns that flash red and blue are hung above the sandy streets, and the scrumptious scents of the food stalls turn me light-headed.

For someone whose world was only a small town and the mines surrounding it, this is an attack on my senses. There's glistening, roasted meat I don't even know the name of rotating on skewers. There's a crowd watching a jinn juggle fire and twist it into strange, mythical shapes. And to my left, a band is bobbing their heads as they beat dreams, shake bells, and play flutes—attracting the attention of snakelike creatures that hiss and curl around their feet. I take a deep, rattling breath. What world did I just step into?

My qareen pats my head when she notices my hanging jaw. "If you're impressed by the docks, just wait until you get to the palace." She snickers.

"Why did you invite me here?" I shout over the fast beat of drums and melodic sitars. This has to be some kind of illusion. But who set it all up? I don't trust my qareen at all. I can't afford to. All the horror stories of jinn swindling keep my guard rock solid.

She squeezes my shoulders. "There's a huge party happening. I know you want to go home, but just stay for the night! It'll be loads of fun."

Just one night? My skin crawls from the thought of sticking around for more than five minutes, but everything I've seen so far has been straight out of a storybook. I just don't know if it'll have a happy ending or a tragic one.

"I really should go," I reply. My feet are already angled back toward the ship.

My qareen shakes her head. "I get it, I get it. You think I'm lying." She snaps her fingers and summons a flame. The fire disperses, and a golden card is left behind in her hand. "Here."

When I don't take the card, she shoves it against my chest. I scowl, opening it slowly. If a fireball pops out and burns my face off, at least I can say I was being careful.

The heat doesn't come. It's just a pretty, decorated card with swooping writing. I can't read much, but I can make out the letters of my name.

"See? Maybe you subconsciously knew I was inviting

you, so you made your way here yourself. Just in time too. It's a night full of festivities! There are prizes to win—worth more than anything you can imagine."

My ears perk up. Expensive prizes I can possibly win and bring back with me to the human realm? My blood pumps with excitement. I might not even need to find the Demon's Tongue if I can return with enough riches so Maa won't have to work anymore. But that's not the real reason I'm here.

"Have you seen my friend? His name is Faisal. He's a little paler than me. Has a mop of curly dark hair on his head. Doesn't talk much."

My qareen shrugs. "He might be around here. We get plenty of human guests."

I bite my lip. Everything she's mentioned sounds absolutely enticing, but the alarm bells in my head still ring. I try to quiet them. I could find Faisal here. I convince myself that's the only reason I let her lead me farther into this unknown land.

I have no idea what this palace is or what's inside, but everyone from the cruise ships and smaller boats follows the jinn in the bright yellow peacoats. They guide us down a stone path, winding into a garden of bright wildflowers and hedges trimmed to the shapes of lions, tigers, and boars. Marble fountains and statues of seemingly famous jinn stare down at me.

"You are now entering the Sijj Palace. Enjoy your stay!"

I glance up, and up, and up until I see towering peaks that practically embrace the moon. The palace is an immense structure of arched and domed roofs and giant twisting pillars, with an exquisite display of the Urdu and Arabic languages carved into them. The entrance is gigantic, and large sconces of pink flames surround it. Vines snake across the outer stone walls, encasing the palace in a mesh of flowers every color imaginable.

I have to hold on to the tree next to me to keep my knees from buckling. I've never felt so small, not even when Maa hugs me and her arms wrap around my entire body. That's a warm feeling. This one is terrifying.

Crows and jinn with black wings circle the roofs as if they're watching the oncoming patrons. When my qareen pushes me past the entrance, I try extra hard to not faint, because everything comes to me all at once—the hundreds of musicians with sitars, flutes, and drums; the dancers wrapped in bright clothes swinging around me; songs echoing across the tall walls and bouncing back into my ears.

Welcome to the Sijj Palace, dear traveler,
can I offer you a mango lassi, a fig, or
maybe a taste of Zamzam water?

The singing intensifies as jinn from all directions offer platters of delicacies and trays of glowing drinks my way. I pick up a gulab jamun and throw it in my mouth. It's heaven amid this hellish nightmare. I'm not even subtle when I swipe two more. I need some comfort.

If you say no, don't worry,
why not dance across the ballroom or dip into an herbal bath,
there's no hurry!
Take our hand and just say the word,
we can bring you jewels, find you love, nothing to us is absurd.

Is this palace always in a state of ridiculous festivity? With the way the jinn in uniform and the dancers are all in flawless synch, I wonder how much time it took them to perfect this routine. It's incredible.

"What is this place?" I yell over the music to my qareen. Unlike me, she's probably used to all the bright blue walls and petals floating in the air.

"You still haven't realized? The Sijj Palace is the most luxurious hotel for jinn that has ever existed."

HOTEL?

I scream when a swarm of snakes entangle my legs and then slither away only to morph into humanoid jinn creatures, breaking into song.

Loosen chaos's control,
take your time, enjoy our service, let us restore your soul.
Stop by when you cross the pink sea,
because the Sijj Palace is the place to be!

This is wild. I try to look around for Faisal, but a jinn in a yellow peacoat grasps my wrist and drags me to the side of the main lobby to register. "You have an invitation from Dura?" he asks.

"Dura?" I try to squirm away, but his grip is inhuman.

"Ah, I think you might refer to her as your qareen."

I turn around and nearly jump out of my sandals. She's still there, smiling at me—my qareen, or as this receptionist suggests... *Dura.*

"Let me find your room." He swerves behind a counter and scribbles my name on a sliver of yellowing paper. Then he drops the paper into a bowl of purple, bubbling liquid, and it disintegrates in a flash of blue flames as it touches the surface. The smoke curls into a formation of words. I don't get it until he speaks. "Space ward, Room 34,686."

I take a peek at the map of the hotel behind him, but it's a barrage of colors and words I can barely decipher. All I gather is that there are three main wards: Space, Matter, and Time. Each one hosts some kind of specialty and has a specific color attributed to it, but my head starts throbbing when I stare for too long.

"First, have a look at our rules and regulations." The receptionist pulls a tightly coiled scroll from a drawer, and with one flick, it unravels and unravels until it's bouncing across the lobby floor and jinn are hopping over it. "Understand? Good." He snatches my hand and presses my thumb against an ink pad. "Just stamp here." He points to the end of the scroll.

The ink tingles on my thumb, burns almost, so the sooner it's off me the better—I wipe my thumb against the bottom of the scroll. The receptionist winds it back up at a lightning pace before I can even make out a single letter of Urdu.

Now it's time to try my luck. "Um, sir, has a human by the name of Faisal checked in recently—"

But I can't get another word out before Dura's hands are on my shoulders, ushering me under swooping lanterns and over intricate carpets the size of the ocean. My head is finally beginning to wrap itself around what's happening, and I know it doesn't like it from the way my gut twists like someone's kicked the lunch out of me.

"Wait—am I really staying here?"

Dura's laughing, but her grip tightens. "It's going to be a

night you'll never forget. I promise. Just wait until you see your room. As your qareen, I didn't cheap out on my most beloved guest."

We're at the end of the hallway, but every room here only has three numbers. I'm beginning to think Room 34,686 doesn't exist at all and these pesky jinn are playing tricks on me. It'd make more sense. But Dura shoves me farther, straight into the wall. I yelp as my hands shoot forward to keep my face from slamming into a painting of a jinn bathing in jewels, but the wall opens like a door, and my heart drops in one quick swoop as I plummet down a slide.

Dura hops in after me, and I scream as we glide down the long, winding metal slide. We pass a banquet of dog-looking jinn as they devour plates of meat, and we leap over a dance sequence as if we're part of the performance. And then there it is. Room 34,686.

"Where's the key?" I gasp.

Dura clicks her tongue. "No need. This isn't the human world." She grabs my hand and places my palm against the door. I feel it sizzle and then, *whoosh*—the door swings open.

It's magical. Not just the door opening by itself, but the shimmering walls that change color with every glance, the floor that seems like glass and reflects an aquarium of glowing fish, and the giant tapestry hung over the bed that depicts an epic tale of a jinn war.

I shouldn't be impressed. I've been *warned* not to be impressed—jinn enjoy luring people to commit sins as they laugh in enjoyment. Countless times Maa has told me to be wary of walking into abandoned houses that might be crawling with jinn, and yet here I am—in a hotel where jinn are welcomed.

The bed is huge. I imagine only princesses have a bed of such size and softness, being that half of it is littered with pillows. But it's mine. Finally, something that's *mine*.

Dura lingers at the door. "Freshen up, take a nap if you want to, but be out of this room soon. The real party is about to begin."

I could use a bath, and that bed looks extremely tempting, but a thought suddenly pops into my mind. There was so much going on that I forgot to ask. "Do you know about the Demon's Tongue? Is it . . . is it here?"

Dura raises a scruffy brow. "De—what? Never heard of anything like that."

Do jinn really not know about it? Is it really just a made-up myth to distract miners from the mind-numbing act of striking dirt?

"Forget about your human worries." Dura laughs. "There's treasure here that can turn you into royalty."

And then she drifts away like a summer breeze, almost as if none of this ever happened. But that's not true. I'm alone in my own room at the most luxurious jinn hotel. Did I somehow die in the mines and this is the underworld?

I don't think too much about it. *Because I can't.* My head is consumed by images of the palace's luxury, the thought of eating as many sweets as I could possibly want, and winning priceless prizes that could help Maa quit her job. And if there's one prize I wish for more than others—it's finding Faisal.

I don't want to let my guard down here for even half a second, but that mattress is calling my name like the gulab jamuns from Mr. Waleed's cart. Maybe if I do take a nap, I'll wake up back home in Meerabagh and Faisal will knock on my door to beg me for a soccer match. . . .

I hear a loud knock to the left and turn around to see a green parrot tapping its red beak against my window.

"Nura. Nura," it repeats in a squeaky voice. "Come play."

I open the window as the parrot zooms off the windowsill and flies in circles a few meters away. "Play," it says again, and then I realize it's telling me to glance down.

A bell rings in the distance. When I look below, my

belly does a somersault at the ridiculous height from my room to the ground. But that's not the worst part. There are lights, laughter, dancing, and hundreds of jinn strolling across the courtyard of the Sijj Palace.

The party's just begun.

CHAPTER 8

Out of the Mines and into the Fire

Come play!" the parrot screeches as it zooms down the hallway. I sprint to keep up with it, jumping over three-eyed cats and skidding around priceless vases.

The drowsiness I felt before has been sucked dry like a crumpled juice box. All I can hear is pounding music and the clash of voices as jinn talk over each other. I follow the fluffy green ball into the courtyard, where it seems the Sijj Palace's night activities shine the most—under the glowing red moon.

The parrot comes to rest on my shoulder, but it's not an uncomfortable hold. It lifts a wing and points to my left, where a large crowd surrounds a collection of tables filled to the edge with different dishes and platters of food. But no one from the crowd eats. Is this a joke?

A loud and peppy voice blares from a microphone. "Registration for the Endless Eating Competition is now closed!"

Eating Competition? I stomp closer and shove past bodies of jinn. It's rather rude they didn't ask *me* to join. Maa always says I might have a second stomach with the way I devour mountains of food. And if I do, then it would be a shame not to make use of it tonight.

"Let me introduce the participants!" the host of the game says.

When I push to the front, the crowd of onlookers are staring at the center of a swimming pool, where the host, participants, and tables of food have been set upon a floating island.

"And this here is Shahmaran, Queen of the Serpents!"

A giant woman waves and takes a seat at a table. Her gold crown is slightly askew, but she clearly doesn't care, as her sharp yellow eyes glare down the food as if it's about to sprout legs and run away. Tendrils of sleek black hair reach the ground, and her scaly green dress glistens from moonlight or sweat—I really can't tell.

Strange-looking jinn take a seat one after the other, an

assortment of spiky hair and stretched limbs, but when the last participant is called, my eyes snap wide open. No way.

"Last but not least, here is—"

"Faisal!" I shout.

The boy with curly dark brown hair whips his head in my direction, and his face becomes a reflection of mine: parted lips, wide eyes, and sinking recognition. Maybe I drank one too many glowing juices and I'm hallucinating, but when I hear his voice, all our memories come flooding back. *Sunsets. Sifting mica. Trying to haggle in the market of Meerabagh.*

"Nura!" He waves an enthusiastic arm. "Join me."

"What is this? Do we have a tag team here? She's a human trying to beat jinn, but I admire her bravery. I'll allow it!" the host bellows.

The crowd of jinn clap and cheer, and one pushes me forward. Straight into the pool. Right when I think I'm about to experience the greatest stinging belly flop of my life, my feet lift off the ground and I'm drifting—like a leaf coasting on an autumn breeze. The green parrot carries me as if I'm paper into the seat next to Faisal. All those feathers must be hiding layers of magical muscle.

I grab Faisal's hand, desperately trying to feel a pulse. And it's there: *bump badump*. He's not dead. *We're* not dead. This may not be the underworld, but it's still a freak show, and now that I've found Faisal, I want out.

"Faisal, forget this competition. Let's go," I whisper.

He jerks his hand away. "Are you kidding? Look at all the food on this table. This is how m much I'd eat in a m-month!"

My heart decides now is the perfect time to do some squeezing exercises, because *everything hurts*. Faisal is right in front of my eyes, and he's alive, talking, even longing for food. And yet he's not seeing the same picture as me. Sure, stumbling into this realm is a little like plunging into a strange folktale. Even I'm a little hypnotized by the vibrant colors and air simmering with sparkles, but the creatures inhabiting this realm are ones we've been warned about since we learned how to walk. Doesn't he realize we're in the realm of jinn—the same creatures our parents spent hours lecturing to us about, because of the dangers they attract? How jinn can possess humans. How they can lure us into performing crimes. How some of them are followers of the devil and want us to switch sides.

But Faisal knows exactly how to shatter my guard.

"Look." He points to one dish. "They have an entire platter of gulab jamun."

My stomach practically screams. Yes, those brown balls covered in syrup are my favorite sweets in the world. And that dish holding silver-leaf diamonds, another top contender. I wipe the back of my hand across my mouth, trying to stop my drool from overflowing. The more I stare at the table gushing with delicacies, the more I start to think staying a bit longer doesn't hurt anyone. Although my desire for food is standard, it's surprising to see Faisal echo my thoughts.

"You're always the one blabbering about safety." I elbow him. "I'm surprised you're not hiding in a corner right now."

"It's not about survival here. Look at this p-place, it's an opportunity! There's a p-prize if we win," Faisal says, raising a brow. "You want it, don't you?"

Of course, the *prize*. My brain went haywire when I saw Faisal for the first time, but now it's catching up. There *is* another reason to stay here for the night—to loot all the prizes in the Sijj Palace and come home rich beyond belief. Aside from reading lessons with his baba, it's the first time I've seen Faisal's eyes glint with determination.

"Oh! By the way, the penalty for..." The host drones on in the background, but I'm busy staring at Faisal, waiting for him to back down, yet he's not moving. He's holding my gaze.

Butterflies swarm in my stomach, and my fingers tingle with undeniable excitement. I clear my throat and utter, "Fine, we'll do this."

Faisal glows at my words, cheeks flushing and a smile

cracking onto his face. He looks brighter than he ever did in our world. I'm glad that he's found a little happiness here.

"Ready?" the host says. Every jinn at the table leans over, about to attack the food like a flock of vultures. "Get set... GO!"

Forget the forks and spoons. I'm used to eating with my hands, and I'm taking advantage of that experience. I grab a couple of gulabs and throw them in my mouth. I barely spend time savoring the taste before I plunge a piece of naan and daal down my throat. Next to me, Faisal looks just as eager, and I never knew his scarecrow frame could handle this much food. Maybe it's because he's just never had the chance.

But in the corner of my eye, there's a jinn with four hands picking up food and tossing it into his mouth at twice the speed. Another one has teeth that rotate like a motor, and all she has to do is slip something into her mouth and it's gone within seconds, ground into dust.

"We have our first loser!" the host points to a jinn who's puked the contents of his stomach into the pool. The host pushes a button, and the jinn's chair springs into the air, sending him flying into the water.

It's a simple punishment. At least that's what I think until I see a giant snapper fish poke its head out of the pool, eagerly looking for more prey. Its jagged teeth flash under the moonlight. I gulp.

I nudge Faisal with my arm, and he nearly chokes on a cream pastry. "We gotta eat faster."

Under the beams of bright, colorful lanterns, I notice Faisal's skin turning green. "C-can't you see me trying?" He points to his stuffed cheeks that look as round and full as the buttered buns in front of me.

No matter how fast we are, or how much we stuff down our throats, the jinn have us beat. They're creatures of fire, and it almost seems as if they have fires in their stomachs that burn food the instant it slips through their mouths. I'm almost jealous. If my stomach didn't scream at me to stop slamming things down my throat, I'd eat all day.

I jerk upright when a snapper fish pounces out of the water and twirls in the air, gnashing its teeth before disappearing back into the pool. Nope. If the snapper fish can bite jinn, then I don't want to know what it can do to humans.

We'll win this competition a different way.

The jinn next to me with the four arms is panting now, but his pace is steady. His arms are sickly thin, really just two sticks, and they struggle to lift anything heavier than a samosa.

"Hey, parrot," I whisper. It squawks. "You carried me

across the pool all by yourself, but you don't look like the type of bird that lifts weights. It's magic, isn't it?"

"Magic, isn't it?" the parrot repeats. "Why, of course it is!"

I lick my lips. Perfect. Maybe the parrot can manipulate weight. "Can you make the food on that table heavier?"

"Will you toss me that persimmon, then?"

I sneak a glance at the host as he springs another jinn into the water. He's plenty distracted. I slip a wrinkled persimmon into the parrot's beak.

The parrot squawks as it flaps its wings, creating a gust of wind littered with red sparkles. They dust over the food on the table to my right, where the four-armed jinn steadily swallows a bowl of nihari. But when he reaches to pick up a pear, it doesn't budge.

"What?" he gasps. He tries again, veins popping along his skinny arm, but the parrot's done its job. The food is too heavy for the jinn to lift. I'd laugh if my mouth wasn't stuffed.

"If you don't continue eating within ten seconds, you're disqualified!" the host bellows. The four-armed jinn's eyes widen. He shakes his head. "I can't lift it. I—"

It's too late. He zooms into the air like a rocket and then crashes into the water.

One down. Plenty more.

Faisal's doing surprisingly well scarfing down roti rolls. But how much food we consume isn't the problem—our biggest problem is sitting right next to him.

The Serpent Queen. Shahmaran. She's the size of my hut back in Meerabagh. The jinn setting new food on her table are struggling, running back and forth to refill the bowls. She yells in a voice low enough to rival the tremors of the mine. "HURRY UP!"

How is she feasting on all this food so quickly? Even if jinn possess some kind of magic, I should be able to see it. My gaze rakes over her body, and it's not until my eyes hit the floor that I understand. The Serpent Queen has no legs because, well, she's half snake. But when I thought the bottom of her body ended in a snake tail—it actually ends with a snake head. She has two mouths!

This has to be a form of cheating, right? Yet apparently every jinn in this competition has some weird skill that plays in their favor. But I can prove that helping my mother raise my three younger siblings makes me smarter than most my age.

If jinn have their own magic abilities, mine is my brain.

Whenever Shahmaran swallows, the scales on her skin lift up ever so slightly and *exhale*. Like a breath. Or a fart. I don't creep close enough to check.

Shahmaran's slouched over, toppling an entire tray down her throat.

"Never tired, are you?" I ask her.

Shahmaran's piercing yellow eyes slide over my human form and light up with amusement. "A human has made it this far? *Interesting.*"

I push my shoulders back and hold my chin high. That's right. I'm not inferior to jinn—just because I don't have magic doesn't mean I can't hold my own. My faith and brain make sure of that. And my brain is working extra hard today—thoughts click into place as I watch Shahmaran's scales flutter open and closed at different intervals. The reason she can chomp down on food without stopping is because her scales allow her to breathe.

I scoot Faisal over to my chair and take his seat next to the Serpent Queen. While Faisal keeps our team in the running as he chomps down on food, I'll chomp out the remaining competition. I smear the leftover syrup from the gulab jamuns onto my hand and run it down Shahmaran's scaly body.

She's too preoccupied with drinking mango lassi to notice my hands. But it's working. The next time Shahmaran takes a gulp, the scales on her body shudder, trying to open. Except the sticky syrup acts like the perfect glue to keep her scales shut.

She pauses, eyes wide, coughing up scraps of paratha.

I can't help my fingers from thrumming against the table. "Are you so surprised a human's going to win that you've given up?"

Shahmaran not only has a big body, but also a big ego. She doesn't consider that her scaly pores are clogged as she sends me a seething glare and topples the contents of another tray down her throat.

I wait. She doesn't even last a few seconds. Instantly her skin tints a suffocated purple, and her slender eyes widen in terror. "What?" she rasps. Sweat rolls down her scales, and even the snake head on her tail hisses in shock. Her gaze travels down her body, to her shimmering scales that shine extra glossily. "No. I—I can't—"

"Breathe?" I raise a brow.

Shahmaran gurgles as her thick hands try to wipe off all the syrup, but it's not quick enough. She knocks over her table and dives into the pool.

Everyone yelps as water splashes upward like fireworks. The crowd backs away screaming. The host gasps. "For the first time in the history of the Endless Eating Competition, Shahmaran is out!"

The rest of the jinn participants are on the verge of spilling too, and one by one they topple like dominoes. Faisal has slowed down eating considerably, but his steady pace is what's lasted us so long. He's popping another samosa into his mouth when the last challenger slumps in his chair, defeated.

"Unbelievable," the host bellows. "A human has won. You two are the winners of the Endless Eating Competition!"

Fireworks burst across the sky, specks of pink and blue glittering across our faces. Jinn carry Faisal and me, throwing us into the air as they cheer. We're spectacles to them, humans who've infiltrated and won at their own games. Pride bubbles in my chest. Winning against Ahmed in our mining games is one thing, but he's a human. Winning against a jinn? It makes me feel invincible.

CHAPTER 9

Sultana

Tonight, you are crowned the Sultan and Sultana of Splendor. Take these pendants and enjoy what the rest of the night offers you."

The host hooks a pendant over each of our heads, gold chains that carry large red rubies. They shine under the moonlight, and I lick my lips. I've never worn anything so expensive. It's an odd sight. Against my matted hair and dirt-stained skin, it feels out of place, like it'll evaporate any second.

"I wonder if these pendants will disappear once we leave the jinn realm." I laugh.

Faisal shakes his head wildly, his curls bouncing up and

down. "You're already talking about leaving? Nura, you s-saw the way they cheered for us. We're celebrities here! *Patrons.* Where and when will we ever have the chance to live like this again?"

As my gaze flies around the courtyard—catching sight of jinn extending trays of sweets, offering me a seat at their table for a chat, begging for a second of my attention so that they can show me a magic trick—I know Faisal's right.

I can feel it in my gut, twisting like a rope, tugging me in all directions.

No matter how much I want to snuggle in my maa's embrace right now, and listen to Kinza and Rabia spin a make-believe story about one of their adventures, and tease Adeel about where his height has run off to, I still want and want and want . . .

It all.

"You're right," I scoff as my lips stretch into a smile. "It's just one night."

Then I realize it's me, *I'm* pulling Faisal out of the courtyard and into the Space ward, past the grand ballroom and cocktail bar. We stop at the Laal Casino, where everything is submerged in a deep red—red velvet seats, red machines, red carpets, red tokens.

"Why stop at just the courtyard, Faisal?" I whisper as I try to catch my breath, but it's been stolen from me as I ogle the vastness and luxury of the casino. "Why not double our profits?"

If I win big, I can have more. As many gulabs as I want, a different dupatta for every day of the week and every time of the day, and any number of soft cushions and pillows to sink into.

I won't stop until the monster inside me is satisfied.

"Sir, how many coins for these pendants?" I ask the jinn at the reception desk.

As he turns to register the pendant, his single eye widens. "The Sultan and Sultana of Splendor?" He gasps. "Keep the pendants! They're priceless. You two are the stars of tonight. We'll provide you with two hundred tokens."

Faisal raises his brow. "H-how many games will that last us?"

The jinn breaks into a smile, displaying three layers of teeth. "Why, all night of course!"

Faisal and I share a glance. We sprint toward the machines, unaware of what rules and instructions they possess. We fling tokens in the air, and the machines slurp them one after another, hunger satisfied as we try our luck gambling.

Faisal's laugh echoes as he runs to a pinball machine and *ping* sounds echo throughout the casino. A snicker escapes me when he loses for a third time. I mumble a quick prayer as I turn the lever on a slot machine. Faisal and I stare at it with unblinking eyes, our breaths stuck in our throats.

Ding. Ding. Ding. "You win one hundred tokens!"

I jump in my seat and squeeze Faisal into a hug. He turns green from my grip, but his goofy smile is still set in place, and I know then that it's going to be a long, delightful night.

We bet on red and spin the wheel on a roulette machine that's divided into sections of black and red. Our bodies are frozen as we watch a tiny ball skip around the wheel until it settles into one of the boxes. And what does it decide to do? Land on red.

More tokens. More winning.

I wonder if this is the "miracle" that so many people speak of. As we pick away the foil on scratch cards, I end up with ten more tokens. Faisal's eyes grow wide, mouth hanging ajar as he stares at the bright red label on his scratch card. *You win one hundred tokens!*

Or maybe it's finally *our time*. For years, Faisal and I have spent days and nights with our calloused hands around a shovel, striking dirt walls. It's all we've ever seen. Dirt. Dirt behind us. Dirt beside us. Dirt in front of us. I could never believe there were lanterns that changed colors with a second glance. I didn't think shalwars could ever shine so brightly, as if the fabric's been woven out of the sun's rays. And I certainly didn't know the feeling of *getting something I wanted.*

It's addictive.

We giggle as we waddle over to the counter, our arms stacked with coins. A few of the red tokens slip between our fingers and trail behind us, but does it even matter? We're rich beyond belief; a few tokens are mere specks of dust to what we already have in our hands.

"I'll have your tokens exchanged for rupees in the morning. Until then, may I suggest a more interesting reward?" the jinn at the counter asks.

I look to Faisal, and his glimmering eyes seem just as curious as I am. We let the jinn lead us out of the Laal Casino and down the hall. There's something odd about the size of the rooms, the hallways, the walls.... Even after I've marched down the corridor of the Space ward for what seems like a minute, when I turn around, I'm at the same spot I was in the beginning. Shivers run down my arms. Is this place... morphing?

I hold that thought as we enter a blue parlor, the glass chandelier winking as I walk under it. There's an aisle of jinn cutting and curling hair, while the patrons relax in leather seats and couches as they sip on chai. But when we get to the back of the parlor, I gasp. Racks upon racks of clothes—the shiniest, the brightest, and studded with as many gems as there are stars in the sky.

"Tonight is special—it's the eve of Eid al-Adha. The Sijj Palace holds a celebratory dance in the grand ballroom. As the Sultan and Sultana of Splendor, you'll be guests of honor, so allow me to...freshen you up a bit. Free of charge!"

It's out of a fairy tale. A strange and more twisted fairy tale, but I'm still experiencing things I'd never be able to do—let alone dream of. Dreaming is something I've left for my two little sisters, Kinza and Rabia. They never got to see the shift in our family after Baba died. Whenever Maa leaves in the morning for work, she looks so thin and frail, I wonder if she'll evaporate in the sunlight the same way a cupful of water does. I've learned since I was little that the world of fairy tales isn't for kids like me.

This is my only chance.

I glance at Faisal, but he looks even more enthusiastic than I do. Maybe he's always wished to be a prince and sweep a pretty lady off her feet. I could almost barf at the silliness of it.

"Don't you think that b-blue kurta is calling my name?" He points to a high-necked shirt with a sequenced neckline.

I could imagine Faisal in it. It would complement his

brown hair, make him look rather bold instead of gentle, but all I can remember is how he mocked me when I drooled over gulab jamun. "Now *you're* the one pretending objects are talking to you."

We begin our makeovers. It's a whirlwind of chaos. I can't even tell what's going on as jinn tug me back and forth.

They first throw us into separate baths, the tubs larger than my hut, with ceramic tiles more intricate than any map of the mines. As soon as I sink into the tub, I hiss. The water is scalding, but it's infused with some kind of jasmine oil for pain relief, and even when the jinn grab their brushes and scrub me raw until I'm red like tandoori chicken, I bite back my tears.

After dirt has been scraped off my skin, I'm seated in a leather chair in front of a large mirror. A jinn with twelve fingers and large pointy nails observes the dark tangle of hair that rests on my head like a nest. I wouldn't be surprised if a few sparrows poked their heads out and began chirping.

"I'll make sure the title of Sultana fits you, meri jaan." She smiles ear to ear as she calls me "sweetie."

She doesn't use scissors to cut. Instead, her nails attack my hair like scythes striking through bushes, and lock by lock, my hair darkens the pearly floor. I want to see what they do to Faisal, and maybe even trick them into giving him a bowl cut, but he's nowhere to be found. I'm in the women's side of the parlor. I just hope I come out looking less ridiculous than he does.

Once my hair is tamed into a shoulder-length sleek bob, shorter wisps curling into my eyes, I'm swooped in front of a different jinn. He doesn't bother with greetings. His yellow eyes are two spotlights, and he uses the rays to illuminate my face as he smacks me with different makeup brushes. At least I think that's what those fluffy sticks are. My mom owns a very small collection of makeup that most wouldn't even consider a collection, but I recognize the lipstick and kohl liner. Then the jinn pats a fat puff full of shimmer on my cheeks.

Every time he reaches back to collect more powder on the puff, my gaze freezes. The powder *sparkles*.

"Is that mica?" I whisper. The words tumble out of my mouth without me even realizing.

"Mica?" The makeup artist speaks for the first time. "It's highlighter, beta."

"I mean in it, like, inside... what it's made out of—"

"Why would I care about what it's made from? Now shut your mouth. I need to put on your lipstick."

There's no use in asking. But I *know*. The mica in that powder could've been handpicked by yours truly. My stomach twists in the way it does when a rickshaw hits a rock on the side of the road and bounces for a split second, jostling my organs with it. How much mica goes into one of those round containers? How many days of work is that? I thought I'd only ever see it in the dirt around me.

"We're done!"

The makeup artist and hairdresser clasp their hands as they observe their handiwork. They share a glance, smiles snapping onto their faces, and then they nod.

"You're ready." The hairdresser sighs, wiping a tear from her eye. "Now go get your finishing touch."

And then I'm swooped into the dressing room, for (hopefully) the final step in this whole makeover. The workers swivel racks upon racks of clothes in front of me— bedazzled, sequined, bright, and shimmering.

"This one!" One jinn throws me a lehnga and pushes me behind a curtain. "Put on the skirt first, then the top, and then drape the dupatta over."

I look at the gold three-piece suit in my hands and try to imagine wearing it. I've never worn a lehnga before, it's something only reserved for parties—and if it isn't obvious to everyone who knows me, I haven't been to many. I try it on, but the second I step out from behind the curtain, the jinn shakes his head and snaps his fingers. Instantly my clothes align. The jeweled shirt fits snugger, the skirt reaches the tips of my toes, and the pink dupatta wraps around my waist and over my shoulder as if controlled by the wind.

"What do you think?" the jinn asks.

For the first time in the past half hour, I get the chance to see myself.

I barely recognize me.

Sure, I am still in there, but my brain is short-circuiting as it attempts to scan my face for recognition. I almost burst into surprised laughter. This has to be some kind of jinn trick, right? There's no way I could *ever* look like this—with silky black hair as if the night sky has been sliced into strands, clear, smooth skin as if carved from porcelain, and dressed in luxury clothes and jewelry I thought only royalty could wear.

"What kind of magic is this?" I gasp.

The makeup artist jinn leans against the doorframe of the dressing room with a smirk on his thick lips. "The kind that comes with money, beta. Hurry now, the dance should be starting soon."

CHAPTER 10

Dance for Me

I'm led down twisted hallways until I stop at bronze double doors. Music pounds against the entrance from the other side like a warning, like an alarm bell that tells me to turn on my heels and run out of the palace as fast as I can. But at the same time, the thumping of drums matches the beat of my heart, and it's as if my soul is already dancing—pulled into the ballroom before my physical body even has the chance.

I push the doors open.

"Welcome the Sultana of Splendor, Nura!"

If my body could light up without being set on fire, this would be it.

Jinn tall and short, foul and enchanting, all observe me as I stroll onto the mosaic tiles of the ballroom floor. Giant chandeliers of flaming candles are glittering above, and every inch of this hall is studded with sparkling ornaments. I thought the Sijj Palace's courtyard or lobby was the peak of its magnificence, but this ballroom puts it all to shame. It's as if someone had plucked the stars from the sky and stuck them onto the dark ceiling, as if flames are embedded into the walls with the way the colors shift like a kaleidoscope. Everything hits me at once— the lights, the orchestra, the intoxicating perfume, and the *magic*.

The ballroom floor clears as jinn step back to circle around me, and the drums hit a lower note, picking up in intensity. It feels like the windows could shatter at any moment, but jinn start humming in tune with the music, and when one grabs my hands and sweeps me off my feet, I realize too late that they're about to break into song and dance.

Tell me, Sultana, how'd you find your way to the top?
Were you chosen, sold, or have you been bought?
Will you hide your secrets . . . like the death of a lover,
to keep our crusade from reaching your cover?

I yelp as a jinn twirls me into the arms of a tall pink lady with two heads wrapped in a bright purple dupatta. Her two heads sing in unison:

> *Tell me, Sultana, we've marched onto your land,*
> *with the help of innocence, we take all we demand.*
> *But you're smarter than most, of that we are sure,*
> *you've set your own traps, except we are those whom*
> *you can't lure.*

I'm barely able to register their words as my feet fumble to keep up. I'm being swirled and twirled, spun and lifted. Dancers are in synch as they burst into high notes, and sparkles of gold flutter into the air as more jinn join the circle. It's straight out of a Bollywood movie—one that's been turned upside down into a twisted performance of the director's nightmare.

And then the circle parts down the middle and someone is walking toward me, dressed in an electric-blue kurta, brown hair smoothed up like a prince, skin shining as if powdered in gold.

"Faisal?" I almost choke on my breath.

The dancers lift him onto their burly shoulders, and he waves to the crowd with the pride of an actual sultan. If he didn't look so much like a real one, I would slap him silly. His dark curls bounce as they set him down in front of me, and dimples pierce his cheeks as he smiles.

"You look c-captivating." He extends a hand toward me. "Dance?"

I grip my belly as I burst into laughter. My cheeks feel warm. He *definitely* should've been a poet.

I clasp his hand. We dance alongside the other jinn, following their flashy hand movements and swaying hips. I'd be lying if I said this isn't fun. It's *exhilarating*.

Tell us, Sultan. Tell us, Sultana!
How long will you last?
The party is just beginning.
If you can't beat us, join us, for a night of singing and dancing!

My heart clamors in my chest, about to fly away with the rapid beat of the music, and all my limbs jitter as if zapped by lightning. I look to Faisal. His cheeks are flushed, his moves are clumsy, but if I tune out all the jinn around us, maybe this won't be such a strange Bollywood movie after all.

The high-pitched flutter of a flute shrills over the music, and the drums quiet, as if time has slowed down. The jinn reduce their singing into a humming symphony, and Faisal and I catch our breath as I wonder what the jinn are planning next.

"He's here. The star of tonight—seen only once every lunar eclipse—the Painted Boy!"

My head snaps up to the giant staircase surrounded by floating candles. The candles burn brighter, flames wild, and everyone gasps as a figure moves toward the top of the stairs. The figure wears a fitted coat, a sherwani studded with amethyst beads and swathed with chains of pink diamonds hanging off the shoulders. The figure steps into the light, and I understand now why he's called the Painted Boy.

The flames of the candles bounce light off his sherwani and across the ballroom walls. He's a walking crystal—or rather, a walking, talking statue. His face is so chiseled I wonder if it's been carved by a knife; chin and cheekbones looking as if they're about to jump out of his skin. Silky red hair reaches to his knees, and his hazel eyes glitter in the low light like pools of honey. But what catches my attention the most are the two horns jutting out on either side of his head like twin towers, ending at sharp points. They have to be at least the size of a flute.

"Blessed night, my patrons," he says, his voice thick with amusement. The jinn around me squeal and bow, as if witnessing the entrance of a Mughal emperor.

As the Painted Boy descends the staircase, he blows kisses to blushing ladies and sends bright smiles to the noblemen who extend their hands for a chance to graze his sherwani.

"You've all been waiting for me, haven't you? Are you that excited to see me?" He sits down upon a sofa at the foot of the stairs, drowning in cushions and flocked by a crowd of waiters who hold out trays of sweets and drinks.

I nudge Faisal in the arm. "What's all the fuss about him?"

Faisal bites his lip. "I've heard the rumors. Whenever the Painted Boy is seen, he gifts whatever outfit he's wearing that night for *free*."

I hum as a smile curls on my lips. Now it makes sense why the jinn around me practically drool at the sight of this bejeweled boy. He's covered in diamonds. But what's the cost? What kind of magic and tricks do the jinn have to do to win the favor of this smug, flamboyant boy?

And...can I win?

"Do you want this studded sherwani?" the Painted Boy bellows as a giant leaf fans a breeze and flutters strands of his red hair. "Then dance for me. The most impressive dancer can have it!"

The ballroom shudders as the banging of drums pounds against the walls. Jinn begin to clap their hands and shout to the beat. Groups start to form, each more eager to get in front of the Painted Boy and showcase their skills. Faisal and I are shoved to the side as five jinn take center stage, arms thrown in the air, dancing bhangra. It's a lively dance of clapping and jumping, and instantly the ballroom is turned into a riot of cheers. Their shalwars bounce in the air as their shoulders jerk and heads bob.

I clap my hands to them. I'd never admit it to the jinn's faces, but it's impressive—loads better than the crazy uncles who burst into dance on the streets of Meerabagh.

But the Painted Boy watches for a total of two minutes before he waves a hand. "Next."

Then comes in the flashiest group of giggling jinn ladies. They move in a circle as they clap to the beat of the drums, singing in a call-and-answer form, and I recognize the dance from the wedding of one of my cousins. It's giddha and I've been pulled into the circle one too many times to be enthusiastic about watching these skipping jinn.

"Hey, little ones, join our group."

A team of muscular jinn with bands of gold around their bulging arms surround Faisal and me. "We do a lot of acrobatics, but our lightest dancers aren't here tonight. We need people who don't weigh too much. Would you be willing to join our performance?"

My brain sparks with excitement, but I wonder if my stomach would agree with being tossed into the air like a slab of meat. Then again, I do love games. And what do I love even more? Winning them.

Faisal grabs my shoulder. "We could sit this one out. L-look at us, even if we go back home with just the clothes and jewelry we're wearing, we'll be richer than the contractors."

The sparkle that shines off my lehnga seems to agree. But the Painted Boy only shows up once every lunar eclipse, and his sherwani must cost a fortune. I'd be an idiot to reject this chance. The Endless Eating Competition, the Laal Casino—everything has led up to this moment. I could go home with a few thousand rupees stuffed into my pocket, or bags of cash heavier than all my mica piles combined.

I turn to Faisal, my eyes gleaming. "I can't do math, but one thing's for sure: if we win that sherwani, we'll be millionaires. What do you say?"

When Faisal notices the glint in my eye, he knows it's game over. He smiles and shrugs.

"It's not like you'll take no for an answer."

A grin whips onto my face. I turn to the burly jinn. "You have yourselves two more dancers."

They explain their game plan as we watch fire dancers spin flaming hoops, daringly throwing the hoops in the air and twirling them as close to the Painted Boy as possible. Heat brushes my skin, and the hairs on my arms stand with excitement.

"Next!"

Our group jumps into the fray. We weren't given much instruction, just to relax if they pick us up and throw us in the air. The muscular jinn start tumbling across the ballroom, performing flips and endless cartwheels. The Painted Boy rests his cheek in one hand as he hums.

Faisal yelps as he's grabbed by the waist and tossed into the air, perfectly arranged hair strewn across his face. I'm barely given the chance to giggle before hands are tucked under my arms and the wind surrounds me. My breath is stuck in my throat as I see the frenzy of cheers and lights below.

When I land in a tangle of muscular arms, breathless, my gaze flies to check the Painted Boy's reaction, and I frown. He's *yawning*.

"This isn't going to cut it," I whisper to one of the jinn. "We need something flashier, something more interesting—"

Then I see it. The thing that'll elevate our performance: *danger*.

It's something I'm used to. I'm not afraid to take risks—I do it every day when I mine mica. So when I see a collection of swords displayed on the walls, I point to bring the jinn's attention to them.

"Think you can fling some swords?" I laugh. The jinn don't refuse. Sharp smiles snap onto their blue faces. We dance our way toward the sword collection, whipping them off the wall and twirling them between our fingers. The Painted Boy sits up at that, raising a finely arched brow in interest.

Once my craving is discovered, I can't be stopped. It's not enough, it'll never be enough—I want to win. Even if I don't need the prize, even if it means nothing to me, I still *want it*. And that's exactly why I swing the sword in a circular arch, the blade glistening under the candlelight.

The muscular jinn are great at adapting. Even if they usually toss other jinn into the air, they're not bad with launching swords either. Faisal merely fumbles with his sword, losing the hilt between his fingers. It's my time to step up.

I try a flashier pattern of twirling the sword. But in the heat and intensity of the moment, when Faisal loses his footing and slams into me, the sword is hurled out of my clutch.

The crowd gasps. The drums fall silent. Time has stopped in the grand ballroom.

Something clatters to the floor and rolls toward my feet. My stomach drops. It's the tall right horn of the Painted Boy. Chopped off by my sword.

His pale-pink skin darkens to a rumbling storm. With the quickness of lightning, he springs to his feet, long crimson hair whipping into the air like a splash of blood.

"You cut my horn!" he shrieks, cheeks a furious red.

My eyes widen. The acrobat jinn all step away from me, dropping their swords. The silence is so deep I can hear the flicker of the candle flames.

"I-it wasn't on purpose," Faisal mumbles. "I b-bumped into her."

I drag a hand down my face. I know Faisal's stutter is just another part of him, but others think his speech means he's guilty. I step forward, a hand to my chest. "I'm really sorry—"

"Do you know how much time, how much *effort*, how much *care* it takes to grow horns as beautiful as mine?" the Painted Boy cries. "I'll have you thrown into the Caspian Sea! Just wait until my father hears of this."

All my patience for this conversation is lost. I don't know if this comes from my distaste for spoiled rich brats, but when I see the bright red pout and angry furrow on the

Painted Boy's face, I can't help but twitch at the urge to slap it off.

"Oh yeah? Who's your father, then?" I sneer.

The Painted Boy trudges forward, his steps heavier, causing tremors to thunder through the floor. He grows taller, hair moving on its own now, sprawled around him like claws, and the whites of his eyes have turned a deep, bloody red.

"The owner of the Sijj Palace."

CHAPTER 11

The Trickster and the Fool

Two jinn in black peacoats escort Faisal and me to the owner's office. Even though I've never been to school, I wonder if this is how it feels to be sent to see the principal.

"When you pass this gate, walk straight and nowhere else. Don't even think about opening other doors unless you have an interest in being lost for eternity."

After giving that warning, the security jinn stay put and push us past a large gold entrance that reads MATTER WARD. Once we step through, my eyes blink rapidly, seeking out light like a fish floundering for water. We're in a long, seemingly endless hallway, and the only lights come from the purple flames flickering in the lanterns that tower above us. The entire area is covered by carpets—colorful, dizzying rugs hang across the wall, and exquisitely soft carpets are layered over the floor. If I wasn't in trouble, I'd probably just lie down and take a nap right here.

I reach forward to graze my fingers through a fluffy carpet and instead reel back with a yelp. The carpets on the wall ripple as if they were water; the entire hallway is like one giant lake that's been disturbed. Even the floor wobbles beneath me.

"This is the Matter ward," Faisal chirps. "Things aren't as they seem. Look at the lights." He points to the lanterns that glow with what I first thought were purple flames, but when I stare closer, I realize it's not fire. . . . It's glimmering rocks.

When I think that's the only thing weird about this ward, I realize how strangely *quiet* it is. There are parties happening all over the hotel, loud enough that I could hear the music of the palace from the cruise ship when I first arrived, but in this hallway, there's not a peep of noise. Another kind of magic?

Faisal is oddly calm as we stroll down the hallway, ignoring the creaking doors across the walls that open and whisper to us. Usually, if we ever got on the contractor's bad side, Faisal would be soaked in sweat, head hanging, mouth stammering open and closed in the effort to think of excuses. But here he seems strangely . . . at peace.

I'm the opposite. All the stories and warnings Maa has told me about jinn and getting on their bad side flood into my head. Things are starting to look dark.

I elbow Faisal. "Whenever your baba told us jinn stories, I remember you hiding in the corner under your blanket. Did you overcome your fear that quickly?"

He whips his head to me and just . . . smiles. "Maybe it was all an act."

I roll my eyes. Faisal might have a way with words, but he's still far from being an actor.

As we near the end of the corridor, we stand before another set of doors.

"Shall I do the honors?" Faisal asks.

I nod. Why is he so excited to meet the owner? I've never seen this kind of confidence from Faisal. It's not unwelcome . . . just unexpected.

Faisal bangs the tiger-head knob. The sound echoes throughout the hallway like the cry of wind, but then the door creaks open and we're pulled inside by the tug of a sweet, bewitching scent.

The owner's office is covered in even more carpets—across the walls, floor, and ceiling. It's like a giant spa, pillows spilling onto the ground, lantern lights low, cushions of every color and size softening the edges of the room. Incense burns in all corners, and my nose feels attacked by the thick smell to the point that I can't tell if it's just heady sweetness or poison that swirls in the air.

"There's the criminal."

As I whip my head to the left, I see the Painted Boy lounging across a couch, eyes half-lidded in scorn. A growling white tiger lies in front of him, long sharp teeth glinting, and probably the only reason it's not pouncing on me is because the Painted Boy brushes his fingers through its fur. His other hand clutches a book with some kind of lovey-dovey scene on the cover that makes me raise a brow. Sparkles shine off his straight and stunning left horn, but when I notice the diagonal slice on his right one that's cut its length in half, my stomach flip-flops.

A chuckle bursts from in front of me, and that's when I notice that under all those blankets and cushions is an office table, and behind it, a jinn.

"I heard you tarnished my son," the jinn says in a low, throaty voice. He stands from his chair, and I finally get a proper look—and feel terror zip down my back and send a warning to my feet to run far, far away.

The owner's skin is lava, burned to a crisp on the outside, but bright, glowing magma pulses underneath, the luster illuminating his eye sockets and nose, and seeping from underneath cracks in his skin. He finishes signing a document with his long black nail, pointed like a dagger, the tip crumbling into charcoal as he writes his signature.

"I . . . we—it's not what it seems like," I huff, barely able to let the words free when his fiery gaze singes me. "The sword slipped from my hands!"

"My son Mirza," the owner grumbles, voice louder now, like the roar of an engine, "is a figurehead, a poster boy for this hotel. Jinn *dream* of possessing horns like his. And yet you, a mere human, unaware of our standards of beauty, think you can walk away unpunished after seizing my son's source of pride and fame?"

Now, that's a lot to take in. It's true, I don't know what jinn find beautiful. The Painted Boy, or Mirza, does seem a little flashier and glitterier than most jinn, but I thought that just came from the layers of makeup packed onto his skin. All of this reminds me that I don't belong here, that I should've swam back to the mines the second I stumbled into that pink sea.

Faisal and I are human; we'll never fit into jinn customs, no matter how closely they resemble us. I remember Maa saying that if humans are made from dirt, then jinn are molded from fire—but they behave in similar ways to us. They can have families, they can pray to our god instead of the devil, and they have their own cultural traditions.

Although I have seen a few friendly jinn traverse this hotel, it still doesn't squash the fact that the majority of them are out to trick and swindle. We're two opposing sides of the same coin.

"Our apologies, sir. If you'd like for us to leave the hotel, then we will. We wouldn't want to overstep any more boundaries," I say, bowing my head. Is bowing even a thing that jinn do? Am I just making myself look even more ridiculous?

Sparks fly from the owner's eyes and mouth, globs of lava splattering across the wall as he erupts into laughter. "You want to leave? Why would I let you leave when you owe me my son's horn?"

So he wants an exchange. I thought being able to relieve himself of pesky human children would light fireworks of happiness in his heart, but he'd rather have something in return.

"Fine. Name it. What do you want?" I cross my arms.

"I want her legs," the Painted Boy cries, red lips in a pout. "Or we can feed her to the snapper fish and have everyone watch!" The white tiger growls in agreement.

I'm trembling now, fingers jittery with the need to punch something—or hold on to. I sneak a glance at Faisal, but there's still that unnerving smile on his face, like his head is in la-la land even though his body is at the center of the underworld.

I grasp his wrist. "What do we do?"

"You mean what should *you* do? They haven't mentioned me."

My jaw falls slack. This is not the time for Faisal to abandon our friendship. If we weren't under the gaze of the Sijj Palace's owner right now, I would be punching Faisal silly if he thinks this is his chance to become a comedian.

"Now, now, Mirza, I make the call." The owner waves a hand at his son to shush him. He clasps his hands together in a businessman gesture, proceeding to stretch his magma skin into a fiery smile. "Instead of becoming fish fodder, would you like to make amends?"

Now, that's something I can do. I've always answered orders from rich men. This doesn't faze me. "What do you have in mind?"

The owner twirls his fingers, and a swirl of smoke wraps around his hand until it disperses to reveal a tightly rolled document. One pointy black nail cuts the ribbon knotted at its center, and the scroll falls open like the rush of a waterfall, tumbling over his desk, across the floor, and ending right above my feet.

"You've already signed the hotel's rules and regulations agreeing to our measures of penalties." One wave of his hand, and the scroll crumbles into ash and disintegrates in the air. I barely got a proper glance, but I recognize it's the scroll the receptionist had me sign with that tingling ink.

"Now you're bound to this hotel until you've fulfilled your compensation."

"What does that mean?" I gasp. It feels like my lungs have been charred and my skin is flaking off by the second.

"Your patronage has been revoked. You must work for the Sijj Palace until you repay the amount my son's horn is worth."

"How ... how much is it worth?"

"Once I find out, I'll let you know."

I slap my cheeks and shake my head. I can't believe this is happening. I have to *work here*? When can I go home? I need to get back to my family.

"What about him?" I point to Faisal. "Can he leave?"

The owner raises a flaming eyebrow. "Why would he leave? He works here."

I jerk back, head whipping to Faisal. "They've already punished you too? What did you do in the few hours when I wasn't here yet?"

"He hasn't been punished," the owner says, shaking his head. "He works here willingly. He's a jinn."

My heart stops for a moment. Is this another trick? Are they trying to make me lose my dignity *and* my sanity? I grab Faisal's shoulder and spin him to face me. That's him—same big, bright eyes, curly brown hair, and round, pinchable ears. "What are you talking about? This is my best friend. I've known him for years—"

Faisal's smile grows wider. His skin begins to pale, shifting hues into a sickening green. His lashes become thicker, and his hair curls down to his shoulders. He swats away my hand, and I gasp when his jagged, pointed nails scratch my wrist.

"You keep calling me Faisal," he says, voice crackly like the flicker of fire. "But my name is Raisal."

My sanity has jumped from the window.

"You mean all this time...you were actually Faisal's qareen? How?" My lips tremble. Competing side by side, sharing laughs as we spun casino wheels, dancing together on the grandest stage I've ever seen...All this time, it was with Raisal?

"Just another trick in a long, long book for jinn." Raisal flashes a spiky smile.

"You're wasting precious working time, Nura," the owner says as he drums his fingers along his desk. "Can you show her to the working quarters, Raisal?"

"My pleasure, sir."

Raisal grabs my shoulders. I squirm, but his touch is fire—scalding, with a grip of iron.

"I'll see you around, human," Mirza calls as he files his nails and strokes the white tiger. The giant furry creature purrs as it sees me shoved forward.

Once we step out of the owner's office, my lungs gasp for air. The dense fusion of sweet oils had my head pounding. I could barely think straight in there. Faisal—where is he? If he's not even in this jinn realm, then have I come here for nothing?

"Did my guest break the rules?"

I whip my head around to see my qareen, Dura. She sighs as if she's watching a toddler spill food all over themselves. I grit my teeth.

"You didn't tell me about any rules!" I yell. I reach forward to grab the front of Dura's bright kameez, but Raisal keeps a strong grip on my shoulders.

The green parrot from earlier zips through a window and flutters down to sit on Dura's shoulder. My breaths shallow. It can't be…Was this all a setup?

Dura raises a brow in amusement. "A night of partying for jinn means a night of tricking humans, Nura. My pet parrot leading you to the courtyard, having Raisal mimic Faisal. . . . It went just as I planned. But when I found out you voluntarily tried to win over the Painted Boy"—she laughs—"it's like I didn't even have to put in any effort."

"Let me go! Where's Faisal?"

Is he still alive? Has he been tricked the same way I have? The only reason I dived into this mess was to find him—bring him back to his family, perhaps even tease his overly worried nature again. The flame in my core that burned with the determination to find him has blown out with a sudden gush of wind.

Raisal scoffs. "Dura helped me trick that runt. You should've seen his face when Dura pretended to be you and told him the only way to leave this realm was to shatter one of the most expensive vases in the hotel. He actually believed a portal would open!"

I squirm in his grasp, the urge to punch the smile off his face growing stronger. The two qareens clap each other's back like they've achieved some kind of incredible accomplishment. My blood boils. If Faisal got tricked like me, where is he now?

Dura hums as she glances at my restless form. "Wondering where he is? Walk with me."

It's not like I want to stroll across the Sijj Palace next to two devilish traitors, but one of them is shoving me forward from behind, and the other won't unlock her gaze from me. We walk out of the tall minaret that contains the owner's office and back into the main building of the Matter ward, but these qareens skip over all the festive rooms and grand halls and instead guide me straight to a stony staircase.

Candles flicker awake as we descend each step.

"I did invite you, Nura, as you are my human counterpart." Dura pats my head. I try not to growl. I'm not her pet. And if she thinks I'm an animal, I'll show her that I'm more a jaguar than a kitten.

"But did you really believe you were welcome here?" She laughs at my furrowed brows. "Think about it. When have jinn ever been welcome in the human world? It's always *stay away from them, don't call them over, avoid kala jadu*—why should we treat you like royalty?"

"Humans have always been so entitled." Raisal clicks his tongue. "They think they're the only ones with brains on this planet."

Dura and Raisal shake their heads before breaking into a fit of snickering. It's an odd feeling to know that Faisal and I would still be friends had we been jinn instead of humans. It makes me miss him more.

We clamber down the last step of the staircase onto a dreary floor with a single red wooden door at the back. The *drip, drip* of water echoes around me. They tug me toward the door, and it has a small barred window to peek into the other side. But it's pitch-black. No candle flame, no muffled voices...nothing. It almost seems like a fake door.

"Why did you invite me here in the first place?" I ask Dura.

They stare at me, smiles stretched ear to ear. Raisal opens the red door with a loud creak.

Dura taps her chin. "If you've wondered what lies past the sea and away from this island, the jinn realm looks similar to yours. The Sijj Palace is a sanctuary—the jinn you see at this hotel are the filthy rich, the VIPs of our world. But there's still people like you, like us." Dura gestures to me, and then to herself and Raisal. "The poor. The doomed. Jinn love to trick, even each other. It's in our nature. We could've bathed jinn in the bathhouses to the east, or broken our backs trying to tend to the gardens and safaris to the south. But Raisal and I, we chose to work here because it gives us a chance no place else will: the chance to trick humans. The rules of the Sijj Palace have been the same for years. If a jinn can trick their human counterpart into working at the hotel, then the jinn can become a patron."

Dura shoves me through the door before I even have a chance to react. I stumble backward and then I'm falling, air battering my limbs, breath knocked out of me—the bottom of this endless pit nowhere in sight.

CHAPTER 12

Curiosity Captured the Mortal

She's waking up."

"Hush down, everyone."

"Another one already?"

Muffled voices curl into my ear like wisps of smoke, clogging my brain until my headache is so strong that I jerk awake. I suck in a fat gulp of air as I sit up, dark hair tousled over my face. My gold lehnga is matted with dust and ripped at the hem.

As my eyes get accustomed to the darkness around me, I can see faint outlines of faces—fiery eyes and spiky fangs, with brightly colored hair pulled back into tight coils. I groan. More jinn. Just when I thought this was my last chance to wake up in Meerabagh and forget this crazy nightmare ever existed, I'm reminded once again that this is my reality.

"Give her some space, children."

The low, calm voice cuts through the waves of shouts. The jinn crowding around me stumble backward, and I finally breathe in air that hasn't been infused with sweat.

I'm sitting in a circle of pillows—probably what broke my fall. But when I glance around at the gray brick walls and low torches, the musky smell and peeling paint, I wonder if that wooden door was a portal and I've been teleported between wards and into a dungeon.

"What is your name, child?"

The jinn with the soothing voice kneels in front of me, a strange birdlike mask fitted over his head, the beak so close to my face it could poke my nose. His skin is purple in the low light, and his long blue hair curls from around his neck to form a braid under his chin. I've seen enough strange things not to question his fashion choices.

"Nura," I say.

He nods, and the other jinn children gasp. They stamp their feet, hobbling around impatiently like my two younger sisters would. "She's Dura's human, isn't she?" someone yells.

"Does that mean Dura's got her patronage back?"

"That's right," I answer. If I can give them my answers quickly, then maybe we can get to my questions faster. "Now, where am I?"

"You are in the Time ward, the basement of the Sijj Palace. In the working quarters." The tall blue-haired jinn extends his pointy hand to me. "I am the Craftsman. I keep this hotel running."

I don't know why I thought every inch of the hotel would be swathed in splendor and grandeur, but I see now that they didn't spend any of the hotel's profits on renovating the basement. Even the outfits here are gray and dingy, and these tottering jinn children don't hold themselves with the same air of arrogance that the upstairs patrons do.

"Let me show you around."

The Craftsman pulls me up to stand, and we leave the huddle of jinn children. He pats their heads as we pass under a maze of pipes, sending encouraging quips when they shovel coal into furnaces while withstanding the intense heat. Every corner of this basement is consumed by the clangs and clinks of tools as furniture gets built.

"This is where you'll be staying." The Craftsman curls his slender hand around a curtain divider and pulls the cloth away to reveal a room of the bare minimum—rows upon rows of small, stiff pillows, thin rags for blankets, and candles that have melted so low they're practically puddles.

My heart sinks. It's not because I can't bear to stay here. This place is more like my hut in Meerabagh, anyway. But when I see the other people scurrying about in this dull room, I drop to my knees on the hard cement floor.

Faisal.

As their heads snap my way to see who's made such a noisy entrance, their eyes widen. But one person jumps to his feet and swings his arms around me in a tight embrace.

"Nura?"

I stare at him as if he's a candle flame, afraid he'll disappear with the first gust of wind. I don't know what to believe anymore. I thought Raisal was really Faisal—jinn have the ability to change shape. But when I look at *this* Faisal, the one in front of me, it's not just his appearance that strikes familiarity.... It's the way he looks at me.

"Is it r-really you, Nura?" His voice is quiet, but it still fills my ears like a warm cup of chai on a windy day. When he stares at me like his whole world has fallen into his arms, I know it's him. I know it's *my* Faisal.

I grab the front of his gray kurta. "What did you say to me the first time we watched the sunset together?" I ask. If my plan is to not let these jinn fool me again, I need to be one hundred percent sure.

Instantly his cheeks redden. His lips open and close, trying to release the words, but I unclasp my hold on his shirt.

It's enough. I chuckle and pinch his cheeks hard. "Why did you get yourself stuck here?"

Faisal rubs his cheek as he sits back. "More like what t-took *you* so long? I got trapped five minutes after Raisal said I had an invitation to this place."

I almost want to laugh at how quickly Faisal got deceived, except I don't want to recall my own embarrassment if he questions how I ended up here. I click my tongue and avoid his eyes, but when my own gaze flicks across the room, I finally realize how many human kids are in here. A couple are collecting clothes for the laundry, some rock back and forth in the corner, and a few stare at the ceiling, eyes hollow. Where did all these humans come from?

"I bet the jinn kept Nura around because it was entertaining to watch how much she believed it all," a droning voice to my left says.

I turn around and my eyes widen. Leaning against the wall is Aroofa, dupatta loosely swirled over her head, lips in a forever scowl. My surprise doesn't stop there—I notice her little sister Sadia is scrubbing dirty pots beside her. In front of them is a boy curled into a ball, face hidden behind his knees. I poke his side and he yelps, springing open to reveal his thick lips and big nose. It's Tahir.

They're here. All the missing children. The kids everyone thought were dead when the mines collapsed.

I gasp. "You guys are okay."

"Okay?" Aroofa drawls. "My life flashed before my eyes when the mines collapsed on us, I can't even remember how we stumbled into this crazy jinn world in the first place, then somehow we're made patrons, but one by one we get tricked into being punished for something we didn't even mean to do. Now we're stuck here *forever*. You call that okay?"

I jerk back. I thought I could work off my debt. "Hold on. What do you mean, *forever*?"

A kid I don't recognize peels from the wall and stalks over to us. His limbs hang when he walks, like he's used them for so long they don't work anymore. "I've been here for forty years. Maybe sixty. Actually, a hundred might be a better guess."

"What?" A shiver runs down my spine.

A girl sighs from the corner of the room, her voice swooping between high, low, and neutral tones. "I arrived just a month ago. But he's right. We're stuck....I can't remember where I came from now. All I remember is the taste of sea-salt air. I like to think I lived in a fishing town."

I don't recognize the girl from the mica mines, and she seems to speak Urdu with a Punjabi accent, so if her memory isn't completely foggy, that would mean kids have gotten tricked from all across the country, maybe even farther out, from centuries to just a few weeks ago.

Faisal grabs my wrist, his brows tilted in worry. "We have to get out of here, Nura. The longer we stay at this hotel, the greater the binding p-power it has over us. Our souls could become attached to this hotel," he mutters, hanging his head.

I look around. All the children in the room are human, and most I've never even seen or met. No jinn. These are human children who've been tricked into spending an eternity to work as mindless servants for the comfort of jinn. I may not be born from fire like jinn are, but my entire body ignites. I'm not going to sit around and let Dura, Mirza, or his lava-lord father force me into a life of labor.

I may work in the mines, but it's for my family. I swallow when I think about what Maa and my siblings might be doing right now. Are they worried sick about where I am? Is Maa working extra shifts? Is Adeel trying to reassure Kinza and Rabia that everything is okay while I'm not there?

Maa begged me to stop mining. But every time I persisted, because what other choice did I have? Yet I tumbled into this jinn realm, fell into their games, and descended into this nightmare by my own free will. The life I wanted to escape . . . of working in the mines under crooked contractors—it's as if I've once again fallen into the same trap.

But no matter how deep a hole I've dug, I'll still climb out. There's no way I'll work for jinn.

"Want to go home," Sadia whines, breaking into tears. Aroofa wraps her arms around her little sister, brushing a hand through her hair. Aroofa has worked in the mines for three years now, but five-year-old Sadia just entered the business a few months ago. By the end of the day, Aroofa's always covered in dirt while Sadia only has a few cuts and scrapes. Sometimes I see Sadia's arms trembling just an hour in, but somehow, she always has a pile of mica by sunset. Perhaps Aroofa might have something to do with it.

And then there's Tahir, with his head in his hands, refusing to look at any of us and the twisted world around him. "Is this just an elaborate punishment? I'm sorry, Maa, I won't let the goat run off again," he whimpers.

I smack Tahir across the arm and tug his hair so he faces us. "Snap out of it. This nightmare is real."

"Why are we stuck here?" Tahir drags a hand down his face. "With *them*?" He points to the jinn children that poke their heads around the cloth divider and peer into our human-only room.

I sneer. Those jinn children...they plan to do the same thing that Raisal and Dura have, don't they? Trick humans so that they can live in luxury. I snatch a stiff pillow from the ground and launch it at the entrance to our room. The jinn squeal and scurry away.

"How long do we have until our souls become bound to the hotel?" I jump to my feet, hands curling into fists.

"Three days."

The Craftsman is leaning against the doorframe, his masked head cocked to the side. "Tomorrow starts the festivities for Eid al-Adha. Whether or not some jinn practice Islam, the Sijj Palace will be throwing its biggest parties."

I suck in a harsh gasp. The fact that one of Islam's biggest holidays is tomorrow completely missed my brain. Even though Meerabagh has little to celebrate, the town still tries its hardest to bring the holy day to life. My heart lurches when I think of my family, the people I'm supposed to be spending Eid with. Yet here I am, a victim of my own recklessness.

"Every year, Eid al-Adha serves as a seal of the hotel's binding magic." The Craftsman holds up three pointy fingers. "This year, it lasts for three days. If you're able to leave the Sijj Palace before the final day of Eid ends, you can go back to your human realm. But once midnight strikes, if your feet are still planted inside this hotel, then the binding magic will take hold. You stop aging and serve here for eternity."

I cross my arms. "So all we have to do is leave the hotel grounds, and then we're free?"

The Craftsman sighs. "Escaping isn't as easy as you think. And to make matters worse, if you're still here after Eid al-Adha, your memory of your life before—of who you are and where you came from—vanishes."

My jaw drops. That's foul play to the point of no return. Wiping my memory means losing everything I know about my family—the only reason that would keep me motivated to escape the palace.

I trudge toward the masked jinn, looking up into his mirrored goggles but only finding my reflection staring back at me. "Why are you helping us? Aren't you a jinn?"

"I am," he replies. He snaps his fingers, and a ball of fire forms in his hands to prove it. "But not all jinn are as evil as you think."

I shove my way past him. I don't need to be lectured into thinking some kind of friendly neighborhood jinn is around me. Time and time again, ever since setting foot in this hotel, anyone I thought could be an ally proved otherwise.

"Funny coming from a jinn who orders kids around all day," I snap.

It's the contractors of the mica mines all over again—shouting demands, yelling in our faces if we aren't meeting mica quotas. I bet this Craftsman does the same.

His hands wrap around his head as if someone knocked

a hammer against the side of his temple. "I—I don't choose who works for me. I don't want children to work—jinn or otherwise."

"I don't believe you."

The intercom of the basement bellows as an incoming order is placed from above: "*Tomorrow's work itinerary is as follows: preparing for the Feast of Qurbani.*"

"Come on, Faisal," I call to him. "We need to make an escape plan. We can find some answers by eavesdropping while we work."

The Craftsman puts on a pair of ragged gloves as he grabs a welding stick. He's working on some star-shaped contraption. I can't tell what kind of expression is plastered on his face, but he hums in amusement. "That's a good start."

I put a hand to my hip. "If you won't tell us the way to escape this palace, then I don't want to hear it."

"I don't know the way out." He chuckles. "If I did, do you think I'd be here right now?"

"Well, maybe I thought you weren't the sharpest tool in the shed."

He quiets at that, laughter dimmed to a solemn hum. "Maybe I'm not."

"Whatever. Let's go, Faisal." I grab my change of clothes and follow the other jinn children as they pin their name tags on their shirts and stroll toward a yellow door.

"Wait," the Craftsman calls. "You don't have to listen to this dull jinn ever again, but heed my words just this once."

I roll my eyes. He's acting like an overprotective dad. "What is it, *Baba*?" I mock.

"Have you ever seen an old man fight for the last biscuit on a plate? Or the smartest scholar in town get into a petty argument over the best book in the last century?"

"That's something a child would do."

"I'll let you in on a secret," the Craftsman whispers, squatting down so his goggles are at my eye level. "Everybody still is one."

CHAPTER 13

Jinn Say, Jinn Do

Need an excuse to throw a lavish party? Just wait until it's Eid al-Adha.

Last night I learned my horrible fate, and today starts the countdown to losing everything. From the second I wake up and enter the Space ward, trumpets and flutes are blasting through my eardrums. The Sijj Palace looked spectacular yesterday, but now that Eid is in full swing, the hotel's celebrating like it's a divine duty. Streamers hang across the ceiling, patrons wear their most bejeweled outfits, and the *food*—it's everywhere I look.

Eid al-Adha is a day meant to commemorate Prophet Ibrahim's devotion to God. Maa told me the story. God asked the prophet to sacrifice the thing he loved most, and as the doting father that Ibrahim was, he gave God his son. It was a test—God appreciated the prophet's devotion, returned his son, and from then on, told the world that humans were not meant to be sacrificed. While animals, for the sake of food, could be.

As I scurry back and forth down the long banquet hall, I see the Sijj Palace took the sentiment to its most expensive extreme. The Feast of Qurbani, or *sacrifice*, is brought to completion with every kind of halal meat I can imagine, platters as big as beds steaming atop the longest dining table I've ever seen. My mouth waters as we pass.

I also can't hide my surprise toward the Sijj Palace. This means it's true—there are some jinn who follow the beliefs of Islam and are allowed to practice it within these walls.

Faisal and I are dressed in plain gray shalwars and gloves as we set down gold platters on the table. This *infinite* table—literally. I can see no end to the rows of seats and clusters of food.

With a jolt, I realize why I had an odd feeling about the Space ward. . . . The only reason all these grand rooms in the hotel feel endless is because they *are*. Could it be called the Space ward because the size of this place is constantly expanding? Patrons can hoard all the treasures they want, and the hotel can host a limitless number of guests if it chooses to...because there's always room for more!

I smooth wrinkles in the pearly silk tablecloth, placing candelabra that burn with pink flames. Each plate is decorated with the guest's name and arranged alongside an entire set of forks, spoons, and knives. I tuck the last red napkin into an empty glass as the first guest arrives.

I hear her before I see her: heavy panting and the whistle of steam as it releases from her pores. It's the Serpent Queen, Shahmaran.

With her appetite, I should've known she would be the first to arrive. The chefs have carts full of food stored and ready in the kitchen. But the feasting doesn't start until most patrons have settled down. Which means not only hungry guests—but angry ones too.

"Isn't it time yet?" Shahmaran yells. A few others join her at the table, but Shahmaran is the only one who looks like she's run—or slithered—a marathon. Her skin shone ivy-colored before, but today it glistens a sickly shade of green.

Faisal hobbles over to pour her a glass of water, but perhaps she's too starving to recognize him.

"You'd think she'd remember the faces of the people who

overthrew her title in the Endless Eating Competition," I grumble.

"You d-did what?" Faisal says. "Are you...talking about my qareen?"

Oh. Right. So all the crazy memories we shared of first entering the hotel belong to me and...*Raisal*. I groan. "I am. You might want to take a few pointers from him. He's a lot more confident than you are. And has better luck at gambling."

"What else did you do?" Suddenly Faisal's interest has piqued. He almost spills the tray of noodles across the pristine tablecloth.

"Well..." I scratch my chin. "We danced together too. He wasn't half bad, your qareen."

"D-danced? T-together? What abou—"

The rest of Faisal's questions are cut off as the guests are seated. A crowd claps to my left, where two blushing jinn hold out their severed horns to each other. I raise a brow. When the two jinn finish the trade, silly smiles plastered on their faces, the crowd cheers.

"What a lovely couple." An onlooker sighs contentedly.

"When's the wedding?" another asks.

Are horns like wedding rings to these jinn? Just like any other banquet, there's gossip exchanged. My ears perk up when I hear different jinn mention the Painted Boy.

"I heard the Painted Boy might be getting married...."

"He was always a bit of a romantic, wasn't he?"

My lips twist into a sneer. *Marriage?* At this point in his life? I don't really know how long jinn live or how old Mirza is, but he still seems way too young for marriage to be in the picture. And not to mention he's one of the most immature brats I've ever met.

I refuse to spend any more time thinking about the Painted Boy. Thankfully, the jinn at the head of the table claps his hands. Instantly the chandelier lights dim, and the orchestra quiets to a hushed whisper of music.

"Let us begin the feast with a few words." The jinn at the head of the table clears his throat and brings his glass of Rooh Afza—a sweet red drink I only get the chance to have during the fasting month of Ramadan—to the sky. "I want to honor the Prophet Ibrahim for his depthless devotion."

He continues his speech while the human servants set platters and bowls of scrumptious food down. I have to wipe the back of my hand over my mouth to prevent the drool that threatens to spill from my lips. Even though us human children are a large, scurrying crowd of servants, none of the jinn even glance our way.

"Are they purposely trying to ignore us?" I scoff as I slam down a pitcher of water. Still, no reaction.

Faisal shakes his head. "They can't see us. The hotel

uses some kind of magic to make all the human s-servants invisible. Apparently, the s-sight of us leaves a bad taste in their mouths."

So whenever I saw something floating, it wasn't the work of kala jadu or jinn tricks? Now, *that* leaves a bad taste in *my* mouth. How many human children have they kidnapped to work here? Just counting the kids preparing the feast, there's twenty of us. But this hotel is huge. If there are human servants in every corner serving every jinn, then these jinn must've captured hundreds of us—and that's not taking into account how many years this hotel's been running.

But invisibility isn't necessarily a weakness. It can be a superpower too.

"I dedicate this feast to the jinn who has brought us all together in such a fantastic place. To the Demiurge!"

The jinn raise their glasses one by one, like a reverse domino effect, as they cheer, "To the Demiurge!"

"Demiurge?" I ask Faisal.

He shrugs. "I only got here a few h-hours before you did. I'm not a Sijj Palace brochure."

I punch his arm. I look to Aroofa and Tahir, both having fallen into a game of how many plates they can balance on their arms. They shake their heads too.

As the lead jinn finishes his toast, everyone clasps their

hands together in a final dua before attacking the food in a riot of whipping hands and gaping mouths. Shahmaran is the first to begin her assault—her tail head slams onto the table and swipes five plates of biryani straight into her widening mouth.

Some jinn pinch their meat with forks, while others shovel rice into their mouths the traditional way: with their hands. It only makes my stomach grumble louder. Now that I'm no longer a patron, none of the waiters offer platters to me, and the jinn that work at the restaurants don't even register my existence. I have to wait to get back to the working quarters to have my plain dinner.

But my head can't wrap around this *Demiurge*. Why did they mention him? And why is he the reason everyone's here today? If he's important, then maybe he knows how to escape this hotel.

I need my questions answered. "How do we get the jinns' attention?" I mutter.

Aroofa shivers as she answers, "The invisibility spell breaks if you have skin-on-skin contact."

Maybe that's why we're wearing gloves right now. I thought it had more to do with keeping the food free of human germs, but it's really to keep us from being seen. Gears start turning in my head.

"Any more gulabs?" Shahmaran asks a jinn waiter

between mouthfuls of rice. The waiter shuts his eyes as she splatters bits of food all over his face. He nods. "Right away, miss."

"I'll get it," I say to the waiter. The only jinn who are responsive to us are the ones that currently supervise our tasks. The waiter points at the back door to the kitchen. "Hurry," he mutters, before scurrying to another calling patron.

I sling my arms over Aroofa's and Tahir's shoulders. "Come with me."

Aroofa raises a brow at the smirk on my face, and Tahir freezes completely. He spins in front of me, hands out in protest. "What are you planning?"

"You all want to go home, don't you? This is step one in our scheme to escape."

Aroofa swats my hand away, clutching her younger sister's arm. "We know you're a hard worker, Nura, but not always for the right reasons."

I step back, my breath caught in my throat. She isn't lying. I know I've messed up before—playfully stealing a handful of Ahmed's collected mica to add to my own, causing the contractors to beat back some sense into him. And then there was the time I tried to sneak flakes of mica into my pocket, wondering why the world was so obsessed with it, only for Faisal to take the brunt of the blame and get punished for it. I never meant for it to happen.

But the chills that run down my back tell me she's not talking about any of those times. I know she's talking about the day the mines collapsed—when I dug too deep.

"I'm sorry," I say, voice quieter than usual. "I should've apologized long ago."

I feel a pair of arms wrap around my waist and see Sadia hugging me, her face pressed against my stomach. "Don't be sad, Nura baji," she murmurs. "You're the best when you're strong."

Aroofa sighs. "So tell us."

"Tell you what?" I mumble.

"Your plan." Aroofa smirks.

A grin breaks onto my face. I link arms with her and grab Tahir by his collar as we dive past the swiveling door into the kitchen.

What I expected to look like a mess is actually a clean, organized machine. The jinn chefs in the kitchen work together like an extended conveyor belt, passing along ingredients and containers. Orders are marked and tallied, and items are restocked and checked. But this is exactly why I grabbed Aroofa and Tahir to join me on this mission.

"Distract the jinn," I whisper to them.

I crouch behind a counter, peering over the ledge to see what ideas my friends invent. Aroofa whisks behind a jinn and plucks a stray hair from his shirt, dropping it into a cream bowl and shrieking, "Hair!" while pointing at the scandalous item. Tahir doesn't even try; his naturally destructive demeanor means he can pick up a glass jar a tad too tightly and shatter it into pieces.

I snicker. They may call *me* a troublemaker, but they're suspiciously good at this.

Once the mayhem has risen like a tidal wave, I glide past counters of mixing bowls and duck under a jinn carrying a tray of roti. When I see the selection of sweets, my heart flutters.

Oh, how desperately I want to snatch every single plate and topple the contents into my mouth. My fingers tingle with the urge. It would be easy—so easy to just pluck a syrupy gulab and let it sink onto my tongue.

Instead I grab the plates of gulab jamun and slide the brown balls into a plastic bag with the Palace's logo on the front. I tie a simple knot and slip the bag into my kameez.

I creep back into the banquet hall. The jinn waiter is tapping his foot and practically pounces in my direction when he notices me. "Where are the gulabs?" he shrieks, arms flailing. I glance at the scene behind him and almost burst into laughter. Shahmaran is throwing a full tantrum, stealing food off other guests' plates.

I throw on my best confused look, the same one I use whenever Maa asks me if I remember that it's my turn to wash the dishes. "I looked everywhere. I can't find them!"

"What?" the waiter huffs. As he sends more children back into the kitchen, I glide next to Faisal and slip the plastic bag into his shirt.

His cheeks flush, and he stumbles back, almost blowing my scheme. "W-what are you doing?"

"Shhh!" I bring a finger to my lips. "Those are gulabs."

Faisal nearly knocks over a cart of Rooh Afza as he throws his hands in the air. "Now is not the time for stealing gulabs."

I smack the back of his head. "We're not the ones stealing them, idiot. I need you to plant this bag on one of the guests."

"Why?"

I smirk. "Do you trust me?"

He sighs. "More than myself."

I pat his shoulder. He looks terrified, with his knotted brows and bitten lip, but he slinks away. None of the guests can see his shady lurch as he picks out a target. When Faisal crouches behind a guest with a crooked nose and fluffy dog ears, he glances my way. I nod.

Faisal places the bag of gulabs under the guest's chair.

I scurry toward the waiter. "I found the gulabs."

He's frantic, pulling at the few strands of green hair he has left. "Where?"

"One of the guests stole them all! Over there." I point underneath the dog-looking jinn's chair.

The waiter huffs, brows furrowed. He growls. "That's definitely from our kitchen!" He blows a whistle, and jinn waiters snap their heads at the noise. He makes a hand signal, and they crowd around the unsuspecting jinn, who's swirling a forkful of noodles.

"What are you doing stealing all the gulab jamun?" the waiter yells as he grabs the bag from underneath the chair.

The dog-looking jinn's eyes widen, and he jumps to his feet in defense. "I didn't steal that!"

"You wanted it all to yourself?" Shahmaran shrieks. She throws back her chair and springs upright, almost hitting the chandelier with her crown. "I'll swallow you alive, you scoundrel!" Shahmaran reaches over the table and grabs the collar of his black suit.

I snicker. Here we go.

The dog-jinn yells and squirms in her grasp. He grabs a plate of noodles and smacks it over Shahmaran's head before her teeth sink into his shoulder. She loses her grip on him, and he fumbles to his feet, running down the length of the table, spilling pitchers, toppling layered plates, and splashing food all over the guests.

Shahmaran hisses, but she's too slow. She tries to slither her way onto the banquet table, guests yelling and backing away, but the waiters are faster. They jump onto the table and run after the dog-jinn, blowing whistles as they shoot balls of fire in his direction.

It's absolute chaos. I love it.

Faisal's jaw is hanging. He looks toward the frenzy and back to me. "This is what you wanted?"

"So naive, Faisal." I click my tongue. "This is what I want."

I shake my sleeve, and a single, juicy gulab lands in my hand. Faisal's gaze trails on me as I maneuver past splatter-painted, shrieking jinn. I bite the tip of my glove and slip it off, my skin finally free.

Shahmaran looks absolutely tortured at this point. Swells of sweat roll down her scaly body, and her green skin tinges an angry red as she huffs over the loss of her precious gulabs. I don't blame her. Gulab jamun can make anyone go wild.

I tap her scales with my free hand. She lurches back and looks at me. Her yellow snake eyes widen.

"You...," she grumbles. A smile stretches across her face. "Impressive little human. You won't win against me next time."

I don't doubt her. But I don't plan on staying here long enough to test that out. "It's come to my attention," I say as I reveal the syrupy gulab in my hand and raise it to the light so she can witness how it glistens, "that you're looking for this."

Shahmaran gasps likes she's just breathed for the first time in a century. She grabs it out of my hands. I smile.

"I can get you more, no problem," I say. Shahmaran nods as she slurps up the syrup that's stuck on her lips. "But I have a question."

"Spit it out," she hisses.

"Who's the Demiurge?"

Shahmaran hums as she swallows. A steady stream of gas releases from her pores like a satisfied sigh. "That's it? He's the founder of the Sijj Palace. He built it, knows this place like the back of his hand."

The founder, huh? That's definitely an important person. If anyone knows the secret to leaving the hotel, it would be him. "Where is he?"

Shahmaran rubs her scaly belly. "No idea. Haven't seen him around in a while."

So that means the Demiurge *isn't* the owner of the hotel.

I sigh. That just means more searching.

Waiters are still chasing down the dog-jinn. Human children swarm the table and take advantage of the situation as they gobble as many delicacies as they can. The entire banquet hall is a mess of broken plates and splatters of food and drink, but I laugh. It was worth it.

I know what to set my sights on now: finding the Demiurge.

CHAPTER 14

Collision Curse

W e're eating good tonight!"

I set my plates of stolen food down onto the cold cement floor in the working quarters, away from the jinn kids and on top of a tattered bedsheet that works as a make-shift tablecloth. Faisal hobbles in after me, trying not to spill the food gathered in his arms. Aroofa, Sadia, and Tahir also join, bragging about their snagged plates and bowls of leftovers. We check our total dinner cuisine—five rotis, handfuls of biryani, some daal and nihari, scraps of meat, and for dessert: half a plate of gulabs.

Faisal sits back with a sigh. "This is more than I ate back home."

It's not the Eid dinner I envisioned. We all sit in a circle, mats folded away to make enough room on the floor. Other human kids are in similar circles, mumbling to each other, shoving food down their throats—food probably more expensive than we've ever known—but their eyes are distant. They're looking somewhere far, somewhere in the past.

Sadia whines as she waves a roti in front of Aroofa's face. Aroofa tries to swat her arm away until something flashes across her eyes, and she takes the roti from Sadia's hands, tears it into small pieces, and gives them back to her.

"You're such a reliable sister," Tahir grumbles. "My baji steals my food when I'm not looking."

Aroofa chuckles as she pours some daal for Sadia. "I just remembered. My maa was the one who ripped the roti into bite-sized pieces for Sadia. But she's not here...." Aroofa swallows, her gaze not meeting ours. "I guess I was so used to having Maa around."

Faisal hums, picking at the meat with aimless fingers. "I used to feed my twin sisters." A small smile quirks onto his lips. "I hated doing it because they always s-spat on me. But today I kind of miss it."

I grip the roti in my hands. This was supposed to be our fun little Eid dinner. Our feast away from home. A gathering of friends and a night to forget the chaos that surrounds us. But it's *Eid*, a holiday practically inseparable from family.

I saw those jinn gobbling plate after plate, the meaning of Eid lost to them. The festival of sacrifice is to give to the poor, to display gratitude, a day to spread love and charity. Yet we're here, kids forced to work for a bunch of rich jinn that have no clue what an empty stomach feels like.

Eid also flew over my siblings' heads—there was never enough of a change in the day for Kinza and Rabia to notice that Eid was special. We didn't eat more than normal, maybe just switching out vegetable curry for a meaty one. Adeel didn't even enjoy going to the marketplace like I did, shrugging his shoulders and saying there was no point if he couldn't buy anything. Maa would seem done with the holiday after performing the special prayer. Even me—I never kept tabs on when Eid rolled around because I didn't realize its significance.

But I feel it now. Overwhelmingly. My gut lurches, and my stomach doesn't seem full, no matter how much food I swallow. Because I'm not with my family, and they're not with me.

Wasn't there a reason I dug so hard in the mines that day it collapsed? A reason besides wanting to find the Demon's Tongue?

I crane my head upward, trying to find the answers

in the dull gray ceiling, but instead I catch sight of three clocks on the wall. The one labeled SPACE WARD has two arms ticking forward, the one labeled MATTER WARD has a dozen or more arms, some spinning backward, others twisting ahead at twice the speed. And then I notice the one for the TIME WARD. The arms stutter in place, like they're being held back from moving forward.

A vein throbs against my temple, and I lose my breath. I try to think of Maa's voice—maybe something she said drove me to dig harder—but my head aches. I really am losing my memories. The most recent ones first. I squeeze my eyes shut, and then it comes to me. Just bits and pieces, but enough for my heart to fold in on itself.

That's right. I wanted my family to eat something nice for Eid dinner.

Dreams don't come to me that night. I wake up with a back sorer than usual and a mind racing with how little time I have left. Two days. Two days until I'm stuck here forever, memory wiped, a mindless servant. I'm not going to sit by and let it happen. It's time to test our chances. Finding the Demiurge is our best lead, but I have a feeling we need to understand more about this hotel if that's going to happen.

Faisal and I are on cleaning duty today, two soldiers in the army of workers assigned to rub and scrape away all the grime in this hotel. The instructions were short but crystal clear: *Everything needs to be sparkling.* I scoffed when I heard the intercom. The sun could be hovering right in front of us, and it still wouldn't outshine the Sijj Palace. I guess someone has been keeping it that way—and those someones are invisible children. They help hide the rot of its dirty ways.

I swipe a cloth against a barely dusty frame and settle the picture of intertwined snakes back onto the wall. To my right, Faisal sweeps the carpet, but it doesn't look like he'll finish soon. This hallway's so long there's no end in sight—just a tunnel of curvy portraits and mosaics hung above ancient pottery and statues of beasts. Countless blue doors zigzag across it, and I almost jump at the sight of a jinn as he steps out of one, skips down the hall, and enters another door.

I pretend I'm not looking, but really, I'm *scanning.* If anyone here thinks that I'm cleaning for the sake of this hotel and its patrons, they're going to be sorely disappointed. Every move, every chore, and every room is an opportunity to search for an escape. I act like I'm swiping at the next frame when the door to the opposite end of the hallway creaks open and that same jinn hops out.

My jaw drops. "Did you see that?" I elbow Faisal.

The broom knocks out of his hands as he rubs his arm. "See what?"

"That jinn." I point. "He went in the door to my left and came out the one all the way on the other side."

Faisal's eyes finally widen the way mine do. He picks up the broom with shaky fingers. "M-maybe it's just a really long room?"

"Let's find out." I sprint to the door the jinn entered through, swinging it open just as Faisal sputters a warning. Music hits me first, a loud orchestra of sitars and drums. I blink once, twice, and yet again, but the band playing onstage doesn't disappear. "How?" I gasp. This door opens up to a viewing balcony of a stage, and the only exit is on the bottom floor. So how did that jinn wind up back in the hallway?

This time, Faisal drops the broom of his own accord. He shakes his head. "Where are we?"

I want to answer with *a demon's playground*, but that would just be stating the obvious. His question does make me do a double take. Where are we *really*? Grabbing Faisal's wrist, I step back through the door and haul him toward the lobby, sprinting past jinn and under their flowing dupattas until we're standing before the answer—the map of the Sijj Palace.

"Let's see..." I hum and narrow my eyes. "There!" A section of the map is lit up blue, with little icons that describe what each room is: a fork and spoon for the banquet hall, a dancing jinn for the ballroom, a pool for the courtyard. It's like it was made for me—written words and I don't mix, but pictures are perfect.

"We're in the Space ward. Here's the icon for the lobby." I scan the multicolored map until my gaze lands on a mini-golf course at the side of the hotel on the fifth floor, right above a lake that slinks into the ocean.

A grin breaks onto my face.

Faisal glances at me, skin turning pale. "You're not really thinking o-of—"

"I am."

And that's how we end up at the edge of a veranda on the fifth floor, the clap of golf balls behind us. The breeze flutters strands of my hair, and the sky is the delicate purple of bruised plums. If we weren't about to jump off the veranda, I might actually enjoy watching the crimson clouds swim by.

"This i-isn't a good idea." Faisal squirms, cupping his mouth as he looks at how far below the ocean is.

"We need to try," I counter. "The doors of the hotel only

lead back inside. Swimming our way back to the mines is our only option. If it works, we'll come back and tell the others."

Faisal sighs, shoulders hunched up to his ears, peeking over the edge again only to shut his eyes. I can't watch this anymore. He might still have a dozen more warnings to roll off his tongue, but we can't afford to waste another second in this hotel. I've already forgotten the names of the contractors, what the latest sketch Kinza carved into the wall of our hut looks like, and why I wanted the Demon's Tongue in the first place.

I grab Faisal's hand and jump.

Wind batters our bodies, and Faisal screams. Seconds later, cool water surrounds us, snatching the air from my lungs. I claw my way back to the surface until my head bobs out. Hopefully no one saw us. Not a lot of jinn were playing mini-golf to begin with, and those that had been were too focused—

Wait.

"It c-can't be." Faisal gasps. "This hotel . . . it's cursed."

For once, Faisal isn't exaggerating. We're not floating in the ocean we dived into. As I peer over the surface of the water, I'm met with the sight of a hundred jinn sitting around in lounge chairs, servers holding drinks on platters, and one jinn diving straight over me. Into the courtyard pool. We're back inside the Sijj Palace.

"The hotel isn't what's cursed," I grumble. "We are."

CHAPTER 15

A Coward's Kryptonite

As Faisal and I head back to the working quarters in soaking clothes, it's a walk of shame. My fists are clenched. All I see is red.

What's the trick? The catch? The strings to this puppet show? Escape seems impossible. I've squeezed out of tunnels skinnier than anthills and dug my way through dead ends. So when I say something isn't looking too bright, I'm not stretching the truth.

I wash up with a basin of water in the bathroom, and then slip into a dry set of work clothes. Every child—jinn or human—is dressed the same. It's only *one* of the ways that the working quarters contrast with the flashy and bright palace above. And the contrast is quite huge—the lehnga I wore the night I was Sultana of Splendor wouldn't even be sold in the same store as this gray working kameez. But there are other little bits of color, strokes of creativity, that bring this place to life. I hadn't noticed until now—can you blame me? It's like suddenly losing the ability to see in color.

As I slip my arms through the kameez, once again looking like an inkblot, I notice chalk drawings across the dull brick walls. Scenes of jinn running through flowers, fighting monsters, and attending tea parties are scribbled in varying colors. I should be checking the log to see if I can find another lead out of this nightmare, but the vandalism is surprisingly entertaining, and before I know it, I'm following the curve of the walls.

The drawings unwind like I'm watching a movie. I catch myself laughing at a scene of a jinn kid summoning a ball of fire only to roast his own hair off.

My giggles mix in with others. Then I hear screams of delight, followed by clapping. I follow the noises through an open door and find a room with a blackboard at the front, and the Craftsman with a piece of chalk in his hands.

I freeze. There are jinn children sitting in rows on the ground, bright eyes gleaming as they hang on to the Craftsman's every word. The Craftsman's masked face turns in my direction, and I almost gasp when he opens his arms wide.

"Would you like to join us, Nura?"

My mouth opens and closes, but my gut is clenched too tight for any words to fall free. Once every child's attention has switched to me and the Craftsman cocks his head, I mumble out an answer.

"Why are you teaching them?" I whisper.

The Craftsman's arms slowly fall. *"Why?"*

My brows furrow. "Are you teaching them how to trick humans?"

He shakes his head and taps his chalk at the sketches on the blackboard, where he's drawn different shapes. "No, of course not," he says calmly, but it only boils my blood hotter. "I was teaching my daily lesson. Today is geometry."

It's all a scam. Education, teaching, learning—those kinds of perks don't help children like me, nor these naive, hobbling jinn kids. We've already been abandoned. We work to survive, not to create foolish dreams that'll end in failure. People like the Craftsman want us to *think* we have a chance, but he'll be the happiest when our hopes get crushed.

I've seen contractors promise the youngest children fake snacks and toys when they weren't old enough to understand the value of money. I've seen Mr. Waleed sell his sweets to the old men on the street at regular price, but when an innocent child with more rupees than usual wants a bite, he hikes up the cost.

I know exactly what this Craftsman is doing.

My hands ball into fists as I yell across the room. "Why would you give them the hope that there's anything beyond this basement for them? That there's ever been more than tricking humans to escape their bad luck? You're horrible." Education only works for people who already have a foot in the door, not those with the door slammed shut in their faces. Not for people like me—and these jinn kids.

The room falls silent. Some hang their heads; others pout their lips as they try to comprehend my words.

Fingers grasp my arm. Faisal bows to the Craftsman before he tugs me away from the room. Only when I hear his voice does my raggedy breath soften.

"Nura?" He grips my shoulders.

I take a deep breath, but all I see is red. All I see are those same schoolgirls back in Meerabagh, giggling and laughing, asking me to hand their pencil to them like some peasant.

"H-hey," Faisal calls again. "I checked the work log. We have a lead. There's a chore to clean the owner's office."

We end up back in the carpet-covered, incense-thick office of the Sijj Palace's owner. There's no better place for me to forget this morning ever happened—because if the Demiurge is such an important figure of the hotel, then the owner must know all about him. The office is in the tallest minaret of the Matter ward, and if you ask me, it's the most mysterious out of all three wards. The walls shift like rolling dice and colors change at every glance. Sometimes it feels like walking through air—as if it's all a shimmering illusion.

With our sleeves rolled up to our elbows and masks shielding against the cleaning fumes, we get our vacuums and dusters ready. I've tidied up my home back in Meerabagh countless times, swiping at the floor when Kinza and Rabia spill food, slapping on another layer of mud when the walls begin cracking, stacking dirty dishes and handing them over to Adeel to wash. What are younger siblings for if not minions to split up your own work?

But whatever the owner of the Sijj Palace was up to last night, it looks as if a sandstorm swept through here.

"Late night Eid p-party, it seems." Faisal shakes his head with a sigh.

My nose crinkles. There are leftover trays of picked-apart bones, jugs of half-drunk Rooh Afza, and the teasing scent of gulab jamun but without any to bite into. Even the carpets and pillows in the room have been shuffled around.

We tackle the plates first, stacking them into high piles. Then it's a matter of finding a nice corner to throw all the pillows against. I may have smacked Faisal in the head a few times by accident, I think. He turns to the shelves and lines up each book according to the color of its spine, and I'm about to gag when I realize he's actually finding this *fun*. I guess it might be.... When you've never had this many belongings, it is kind of nice to just organize things and hum at the satisfaction of it all looking pretty.

I call it quits after that, shutting off the vacuum and spinning to face Faisal. He stops at the sudden lack of noise, and halts his feather duster mid-swipe.

"L-let me guess." He groans. "You're done cleaning?"

I roll my eyes. "That's not what we came here to do. While you were busy lining up every book by color, I was scanning the room for hints. And look!"

I point at the corner where we've thrown the enormous pile of pillows. Behind the pile are three doors—yellow, red, and blue. I yank the red door open. It's pitch-black inside.

"I wouldn't try stepping into that..." Faisal jerks away.

My eyes widen. When Dura led me down the staircase, she shoved me through a red door that also had nothing but eerie darkness behind it. And when I awoke, I was in the working quarters. The Time ward. I have no interest being back down there.

I jump to the next door, blue with rounded edges and a gold doorknob. I lick my lips. "Let's try this one."

Faisal gasps. My jaw drops. Behind this door is the night sky, stars and swirling galaxies swimming amid negative space. That's it! This must be the way to the Space ward.

Faisal jumps to the last yellow door before I get the chance. It shines like metal, so smooth we can see our reflections. Faisal takes a deep breath before pulling it open.

We stare at the strange illusion in front of us. It's like we've pulled back the curtains to a giant oil painting, smears of vivid, clashing colors spiraling against each other. With every blink I take and every angle I shift, it transforms. One second a mixture of blues and reds, and the next, a trippy splatter of purple and green. The Matter ward.

I reach out before Faisal can stop me.

"Nura, what are you—" His yell cuts off as the same shock that shudders through me strikes him as well. Half of my arm is in the office, and the other half inside the odd oil painting.

"These are portals," I breathe. "Now it all makes sense."

It's not a curse—it's magic. From the outside, the hotel

looks like just one giant building, but it's not attached at all. . . . Almost as if each ward lies in a different dimension, connected only by portals.

"It's worse than I thought." I tug my arm back with a groan and slam the door shut. "How on earth are we supposed to find an exit when we might not even be in the right *dimension*?"

"G-giving up?"

I scoff. "As if. You know better than anyone else that I'm a hard worker. Haven't my mica earnings shown you that?"

"You mean you only w-work hard w-when there's something to gain. With mica, it's money. In this office, it's information about the Demiurge."

It's crazy how well Faisal knows me. He should've been my qareen. . . .

"I like it when you use your brain," I say, springing onto a couch. "So what do we know about the Demiurge?"

"You said he was the founder of the Sijj Palace."

Now that I've discovered the strange mechanics of the hotel, escaping doesn't seem like something humans are even able to *imagine*. We'd need a jinn's brain to help us— and not just any jinn. "If he built it, don't you think he'd know the secret to escaping?"

"Well, then what about this?"

Faisal points his feather duster at the picture frame he

just wiped. It's an old photo of the owner, in all his glowing magma glory, with an arm around another jinn. The other jinn looks friendly, with ashy gray skin like the slag of a volcano, and they're both wearing hats that display the Sijj Palace's logo. In the back I see it—the hotel. It's lacking the vibrance of the colorful lights and lavish mosaic decorations, but the foundation is there.

Faisal reads the label under the photo: "*The Demiurge, Founder of the Sijj Palace, with Majoon, the Hotelier of the Sijj Palace.*"

"They knew each other. Heck, they were chummy," I comment as I raise a brow. So why hasn't the Demiurge been seen recently?

I glance around the room. The intricate carpets look clean enough. We've opened the shutters to release the heavy smell of the incense sticks and placed new ones in their holders. The only thing left in this office that's still messy is the owner's desk.

Documents are spilling out of the drawers and cabinets, and stacks of teacups with varying levels of leftover chai are littered across the top. I huff and roll up my sleeves once again. There's a reason I'm Ahmed's number one rival when it comes to mica collecting. Others may collect more flakes than I do, but I don't bother with every tiny speck. I go for statement pieces—big hauls. I pick out what really matters.

I lunge for the desk. I sift through the documents on top, scanning for anything close to the word *Demiurge*—Faisal tells me what to look for. When I don't see the jumble of letters that spell out the title, I throw the useless documents in his direction. I'm ravaging through this desk like a vulture tearing at meat while Faisal licks the bones clean after me.

It seems to be just regular boring business documents. The owner sounds like a busy man. Then why is Mirza, the Painted Boy, such a sloth in comparison? Some parents must be blind in the face of affection.

Nura, I don't want you working in the mines anymore.

I hear Maa's voice. Yeah, some parents are blind in the face of affection. But I'm blind in the face of shiny, glistening sweets. We all have our weaknesses.

When I jiggle the drawer open to search for more papers, I find what I'm looking for: the word *Demiurge* written in bright red letters.

"Faisal." I wave my hand for him to come closer. "Can you read it?"

He swallows. Faisal's never had formal education either, but his baba knows how to read and write, and on more than one occasion has tried to teach us. Faisal would sit patiently as his baba inscribed words on a small chalkboard, while I lounged on their cot watching the sun slink down the horizon. I didn't need any more reasons to crave an education. I didn't want to wish for something I'd never be able to get.

He looks like he's about to refuse, but I shove it closer to his face. I don't care if he pronounces half the words wrong or stutters every three seconds. "If you can do it, we could get out of here."

He takes the papers with a shaking hand. I know he's not the most confident boy—he never has been. When I asked him what his thoughts were about school, he just shrugged with a sheepish smile. *Maybe it's b-better that I can't go. If I could, people would find my s-stutter annoying, wouldn't they?*

Throughout our years of mining mica, he's kept a low profile. Even though the best mica collectors are discovered within a few days of working, everyone's at least *tried* to see if they could rank at the top. Ahmed was already number one when I joined, but I dug diligently to earn my second place. So when Faisal started working a few weeks after me and dropped his shovel, panting heavily after the first few strikes, I didn't question why he didn't try to play our games. It's not that he wouldn't—it's that he couldn't.

But this isn't mining mica. This is something he *can* do. It's something he has the skills for.

I squeeze his shoulder. "Just pretend your baba is grading your reading skills."

He glances at me for a moment, then nods. I wonder if he misses his family just as much as I do mine. It's the thought of them that's pushing me forward, and when I see the glint of fire in his eyes, I know he feels the same. His gaze roams the document, lips opening and closing as he reads silently. "The Demiurge is on a work trip...but there's no return date."

I scoot closer to him and eye the document as if it makes sense to me. "Are you sure?"

A nervous smile melts onto his face as he locks gazes with me. "Do you trust me?"

I scoff, rolling my eyes. "More than myself."

Faisal's smile is a little more confident after that. He places the document back inside the drawer and shuffles the remaining papers into neat piles. "He's been gone for over a decade, Nura."

My brows lift to the edge of my forehead. "A decade? But where? Why? Wouldn't he want to oversee the development of his own hotel?"

Faisal shrugs. "It doesn't hint at anything. If I can offer my best guess...I d-don't think the Demiurge is going to come back."

"No!" I spring to my feet and slam my fist against the desk. "How else are we supposed to escape?"

"What's this about escaping?"

I hear the bubble and hiss of lava. I feel the heat of flames. And then I see him—Majoon, the owner of the Sijj Palace—enter his office. My head snaps to look at the wall clock. Dang it. I wasn't keeping track of time. We were supposed to have finished cleaning, packed away our supplies, and exited the room twenty minutes ago. Which would explain the burning frown on the owner's face right now.

"Escaping?" I chuckle nervously. "I meant leaving this room—"

With a flick of his finger, the owner burns my lips shut as if they were welded together. "Mmph!" I mumble. I scratch frantically at my mouth to get it open, but it's useless.

"I wasn't asking you." The owner sets his gaze on Faisal. Faisal clasps his hands together and steps away from the desk. "It doesn't appear to me that you two were cleaning. Tell me, then, what *were* you doing?"

Faisal glances at the floor, then to me, then back down. He fidgets with his fingers and shuffles his feet aimlessly. I want to yell at him to just say something, *anything*—it'd be better than the thickening silence that's pinning us down into the coffin of this room.

"Well?" the owner asks.

It's always been like this. Whenever the contractors scolded us for digging less mica than the day's standard, I'd cross my arms in defiance and show them the blood under my nails to prove my efforts. But Faisal just stood there and took their abuse without a single whimper. I used to think it was because he was strong and mature enough not to complain, but now it dawns on me why exactly he refused to say a word.

"Domb fhe agh gowurgh!" I yell behind tightly shut lips. *Don't be a coward.*

He sneaks a glance at me with tilted brows. Even if he doesn't understand my jumbled words, he can read the message I'm sending through my eyes. *Lie. Make up an excuse.* It's the only way the owner might let us off the hook. It's the only way we won't lose more precious time.

Faisal just shakes his head.

The owner crosses his arms. "Snooping around my office is deserving of punishment. Your next duty will be to clean out the coal furnaces. All one hundred of them."

If my lips weren't sealed shut right now, my jaw would be hanging. Shoveling all the soot and scraping the char out of a hundred coal furnaces will take us the rest of the day, not to mention turn us into walking burnt skewers. We'll only have tomorrow left to find the secret to escaping. Even if my heart tells me it's still possible, with the way sweat rolls down my neck, my body seems to think otherwise.

CHAPTER 16

Those That Are and Those That Become

I can't take it anymore.

It's like I haven't breathed fresh air in a hundred years. The coal fumes and the stench of dirty children rile the worst of headaches out of me. It's been hours of scrubbing the cement floor and the charred insides of the furnaces, hissing at the lingering heat that makes my skin feel like it's melting off. I really do look like a burnt skewer. I'm covered head to toe in black soot.

Someone take me back to the mines.

Don't get me wrong. The mica mines are a less-than-favorable job. But working alongside my friends, playing our stupid little games, and being able to come home to my family are things I miss dearly. Luxuries. The Sijj Palace's working quarters are a dungeon in comparison.

I'm missing it a lot more knowing that I might not have these memories after tomorrow.

As I shovel out the ashes in the last furnace and replace it with a fresh set of coal, I head back to the supply room for a change of clothes. My feet stop in their tracks when I see Aroofa with her head in her hands, shoulders shaking like an earthquake, Tahir patting her arm to no success.

I scurry toward them, brows raised from surprise. I've never seen Aroofa cry. Most people think *me* tough, blood under my nails and layers of dirt caked onto my skin without a care in the world, but I've still cried out of frustration a few times. Yet ever since Aroofa joined, not a single tear has stained her face. If someone told me she was born without tear ducts, I'd probably believe them.

A scowl twists my lips. I turn on Tahir, arms crossed. "What did you do?"

"Nothing!" He jerks back, shaking his head wildly. "It's actually..." He drags a hand down his face, eyes wide, and my stomach lurches like a tidal wave. Tahir's a goof, always more sleepy than awake, not a worrying bone in his body.... So why does he look so serious?

It's at that moment Faisal joins us, glancing between us

all. If I can feel this blanket of worry, he's probably buried by it.

Aroofa sniffles, rubs her face, but when her hands drop, I suppress a gasp. Her eyes are bloodshot, snot smeared over her upper lip, scarf draped crookedly. "Sadia doesn't remember me."

"What d-do you mean?" Faisal fidgets with his fingers.

Aroofa's voice is raspy; too much crying has scratched away her throat. "She's lost her memories of me." A hiccupping sob bursts from her mouth, but she does her best to swallow it. "She's so young that she doesn't even have a lot of memories to begin with, but... I called her name. A and she asked me who I was."

Words leave me. My mouth stutters open and closed, and it's like I'm a fish out of water, gasping for breath instead of trying to make sense of it all. But there's nothing to make sense of. Little Sadia has lost memories of her older sister. She probably has no idea why she's here in the first place. Who and what jinn are. For a second I think maybe it's better she stays in the unknown, blissfully unaware of the horrible predicament we're in. But Aroofa's heart is ripped open and the pieces are fallen between us.

What if I start forgetting Kinza and Rabia? Their bright laughter that wakes me like an alarm? What if I forget the adrenaline of wrestling Adeel to the ground and the way

Maa breaks us apart when he starts whining? And Maa's hugs... What if I forget her hugs?

"Aroofa." Cold sweat washes over me, but my gut is burning. We can't stay here any longer. We can't afford to. I march forward and grab her shoulders. "I'll get us out of here."

My voice breaks at the end of that sentence. I don't want anyone to see me like this. I grab a fresh set of clothes and storm out of the supply room. I need to get out of here. I need to escape. I need to move forward. I need to—

"Nura!"

Faisal makes no effort to look at me. His head droops like a wilting flower, and usually at this point I'd shower him with a bit of praise to get him blooming again, but he needs to know what he just cost us. If he'd just lied to the owner about our snooping, we wouldn't have wasted so much time scraping ashes out of furnaces. How did he finish cleaning at the same time as me? In the mines, I usually dig twice his haul. Yet here he's somehow caught up to my speed.

"Sounds like you're working harder here than you do in the mines," I snap. "Lost the will to leave?"

Faisal glances up with wide eyes. His lips part, but I've snatched the words from him.

"I only came here for you, Faisal. I dug until night, almost got mauled by jinn on the way to the palace, and then fell into this trap all so I could take you back home." My chest heaves, fingers twitching with the urge to punch something. "Yet you couldn't even say one word to the owner this afternoon? Look at where it got us. We've spent hours breathing in soot instead of searching for the Demiurge!"

Faisal's hands tighten against the hem of his kurta as he takes a step closer to me. "You never listen to anyone but yourself. Did you forget my warning that d-day? I *told* you not to dig deeper. And what happened? The mines collapsed."

I swallow a lump in my throat. Icy pricks needle down my back, as if someone's dumped a bucket of freezing water over me. Faisal's never outed anyone before, *even* when they've done questionable things. I almost want to clap his back with pride, but when the accusation is against me, it hurts ten times more coming from him.

And then without moving an inch, he slaps me with his words. "It's because of you that we're in this mess."

Heat bubbles in my chest, my eyes are stinging, and every vein in my body feels like it's about to snap. I want to fling an insult as easily as I always do, but my lungs are sandbags with no room to breathe. I sprint past him. It's like I'm a barrel tumbling downhill. I don't want to see, talk, or listen to anyone for the next—

"Ow," I yelp as I slam into a body, one much taller than my own, and far warmer, as if fire runs through their veins and not blood. Oh. I should've known it was a jinn.

"Already done?"

I glance up and see the Craftsman, his circular goggles staring back at me. I can never really get used to his bizarre mask—it's like talking to a demon dressed in a hazmat suit. But then I wonder which is worse: a demon or a jinn? If these are the kinds of questions I'm asking, I must have really screwed up.

"Are you going to order me to do something else now?" I place my hand on my hip.

"Come with me," the Craftsman says as he turns a corner and walks under a plastic divider.

I'm not in the mood to entertain the Craftsman, especially after I caught him teaching this morning. But it's either following him or having to answer Aroofa and Tahir, or worse, facing Faisal once again. I cross my arms with a scowl and follow.

"This basement is in the Time ward, which means it's a place where time shifts and contorts, almost like a balloon. It causes memories to fade and people to never age. Even

I've forgotten how long I've been stuck here," the Craftsman whispers.

When I creep under the divider, I gasp.

All around me are glittering metal stars hanging from the ceiling on translucent strings. A glowing yellow moon is pinned high at the rear of the room. Mountains and forests are painted on the walls with such detail I think I've stepped outside for a second. But I haven't—this room is just one beautiful delusion.

"I don't remember the last time I've been outside," the Craftsman murmurs.

Without windows here in the working quarters, time is difficult to keep track of. I can see why the Craftsman's memory would be muddled.

"Do you remember?" He turns to face me. "What the air tastes like?"

I slump down to the floor, gazing at the night sky—or the imitation of it. "Tastes like?" I whisper. "It tastes like a river that's traveled many places, fused with foreign flavors from across the world."

The Craftsman hums. He flips a switch and a second layer of stars illuminates, creating flickering constellations. "And the soil beneath your feet? Do you remember what that feels like?"

I know it all too well. When I think about the sparkling

dirt surrounding my town of Meerabagh, my heart swells with a sudden longing for it. "Yeah. It feels like stepping on the dough my maa makes to cook roti."

The Craftsman chuckles at that. "How about the smell of an early morning? When the sun has barely risen?"

I close my eyes and smile. I've always woken at the crack of dawn to start mining, hit with the commotion of shouting kids and shovels clanging. "Smell?" I snicker. "It smells like the start of chaos."

"Chaos?" the Craftsman asks in a quiet voice, as if talking to himself. He's sitting against the wall, under a painting of a large willow tree. "What if I told you that chaos is the only truth of this world?"

I shrug. "I wouldn't understand you."

"Those that are and those that become," the Craftsman whispers. The glimmer of the stars reflects off his goggles and winks at me. "These are the only two possibilities. What always changes and never is, and what always is and never changes."

"If you're so intelligent," I drawl, rolling my eyes, "then why don't you tell me my probability of escaping this palace?"

The Craftsman strokes his mask, pockets of starlight dancing across it. "I haven't been able to leave this place in years. The *idea* of escaping has never left me, never changed. But *actually* escaping is just a mere wish...a challenge that constantly transforms. As I said, some things always are, without ever becoming. Some things become, without ever being. The world only provides questions and rarely ever the answers. And in our world, you shouldn't hope for anything more than a likely story."

"So what?" I scoff, trying to make sense of his words. "You're telling me to just give up?"

"I didn't say that. Sometimes, concepts can be more real than the objects that imitate them. Ideas are immortal; they belong to an eternal world. But our opinions, our wishes, they reside in this physical world, prone to become or change. Tell me, what is escape to you? What does it look like? It's hard for you to see it, because you don't know the way out. Only once we see the right picture can escaping become a more possible task. It's not wrong to look at an ideal image and find what you are truly seeking. Escape seems like the only answer. But can you dig a little deeper?"

I'm speechless. It's the first time someone's sent words of encouragement my way. Or rather, it's the first time an adult has seen my worth past quick hands and calloused feet. Maybe I'm just astonished by the way the Craftsman spoke those last few sentences, as if he was short of breath, as if it strained him to let the words free. There's history in these walls, a history between the Craftsman and the Sijj Palace, but I don't dare ask.

"Dig? I can do it. I'm the best mica miner in all of Meerabagh."

He hums. "Tomorrow's the last day of Eid, isn't it?"

"Yeah." I'll finally be able to resume my investigation. But with only one day left, do I really have a chance like the Craftsman says I do?

"Then set this up in the parlor for me." From the back of the room, he lugs out a giant contraption covered by a white sheet. His pointy fingers grasp the cloth and pull it away—unveiling a humongous, brilliant, star-shaped chandelier. It shines from within like a glowing sun about to explode. It's as if he's plucked a real star out of the night sky and handed it to me.

"This... you were working on this when we first met, weren't you?" I ask. My voice is more breath than it is sound.

He nods, chuckling. "So you weren't in such a red rage that you noticed what was going on around you?"

I cross my arms, trying to stop my lips from quirking upward. Sometimes I'm stubborn to the point where I'd jump off a cliff just to spite those around me. It's in my blood.

He strokes the star chandelier with a softness I only reserve for the stray kittens that prance down my street. "I like recreating objects of nature. It helps me remember what they look like...what they feel like. I'm sure those in the parlor will enjoy this too. I'll tell a few others to help. This chore might be more useful than you think."

"Is this...Are you helping me?" I step forward.

"I better get back to work," he says, checking his wrist-watch. I raise a brow. How does he tell time with that thing when there are six arms running at five times normal speed poking out in every direction?

There's no point in pressing him for an answer. He's just going to twist his words like a labyrinth again, and I could use a few more minutes ogling the wonder in this room. Even though it's nothing but an imitation of the world at night, it's comforting—much more comforting than the grungy gray of the rest of the working quarters. But when my gaze slides across the paintings on the walls and I see the faint image of the dazzling Sijj Palace behind a lake of boats and cruise ships, I sit up with my breath caught in my throat.

"Do you know anything about the Demiurge?"

His back is turned to me, one hand already reaching

for the plastic divider, but the Craftsman halts. "I haven't heard that name in a while."

"Well?"

He cranes his head to face me, but that mask hides everything.

"The Demiurge is gone. And I don't think he'll ever be back."

CHAPTER 17

Endless Cycle

When the Craftsman said, *I'll tell a few others to help*, I wasn't expecting to be side by side with a tiger-toothed jinn and across from a bright yellow monstrosity. Faisal, Aroofa, and Tahir are also a part of the team, but it's the first time us humans and jinn have to work together, in *harmony*. And as expected, we're not doing so well.

"Put your back into it," I grunt to the yellow jinn with a shimmering blue sheen of sweat across his forehead.

"Can't you see I'm trying?" he whines.

The Craftsman's star chandelier must weigh more than a baby elephant. The pointy end digs into my shoulder, ripping a groan from my throat. Everyone else is in the same state of distress, as we each carry one end of the six-pointed star across the palace. Faisal almost tripped over the potted plants in the garden, costing us our entire trip, but Tahir was even worse—he'd been one centimeter away from poking out his own eyeball with the tip.

The jinn children assigned to this task are surprisingly competent, or maybe that's not as surprising as I'd like to think. I've always assumed jinn only like to swindle and take advantage, letting others do the dirty work, but I can see their skills come from experience—working at this hotel far longer than us humans have. They know the ins and outs, the shortcuts, and which jinn to avoid as we pass by some snooty, loose-lipped aristocrats.

"All right, we just have to get past this door," I wheeze.

I knock on the mosaic glass door of the parlor. For the first time in a while, I don't scowl at the jinn in front of me. It's the hairdresser with the razor nails who helped me with my makeover.

I breathe a sigh of relief. "Hey—"

"Come in."

Her words are as cold as an ice bath. When she turns around and walks back into the parlor, I can't help but stick out my tongue behind her back. Aroofa elbows me in the arm.

We drag the chandelier with pants and groans, stopping at the center. It's a vast space of marble tiles, vines snaking across the walls, and jinn occupy lounge chairs, tanning beds, or leather sofas as they hold out their hands to get manicured.

There's a small opening in the ceiling to fasten the head of the dangling chandelier to. But there's one big problem. I'm barely five feet tall, and the rest of our ragtag group are only one or two inches taller than me—while that ceiling, well, it's about as high as a two-story building.

"There must be a ladder around here," I grumble, scanning the room. I elbow the tiger-toothed jinn next to me. "Can't you ask around? The workers here don't seem very human-friendly."

"I have a name, you know. Sughal. Remember it." A scowl stretches across his face, and I realize just how long his fangs actually are. Maybe I will remember it.

Sughal whips his head back and forth. "I'll ask—wait. Isn't that . . . Dura and Raisal?"

My tired limbs instantly jolt awake when I hear those names. I follow his line of sight toward two lounge chairs occupied by jinn with creamy face masks and cucumbers over their eyes, a platter of fresh fruit between them.

Perhaps it's because our positions are switched, or it's just their uncanny resemblance to us, but blood pumps through my veins with a ferocity reserved for marathons. I can't stop my feet before I'm trudging over to the imposters and slapping the cucumbers off their faces.

Dura sits up in a flash, a snarl twisting her lips. When her gaze settles on me and a smirk replaces it, it only strikes my galloping heart harder. "Here to rinse off my face mask?" she asks.

"I'll rinse off more than just that," I snap.

Aroofa grabs my arm and tugs me away from Dura, but my seething glare is already latched on. Faisal, on the other hand, avoids Raisal like the plague, backing away from the wicked grin the jinn boy flashes.

"It's been a while," Sughal exclaims, clutching his chest while he regards Dura and Raisal with glittering, awed eyes. "When we heard you guys got made patrons, you lit a spark in us all. You're my inspiration."

I reel backward. "Inspiration?" I yell. "So tricking humans into a life of labor is a source of *pride* for you?" I knew jinn were bad, that they could be treacherous, sneaky creatures, but the Craftsman had me hoping that wasn't the case for them all. Yet here we are, my suspicions once again proven right. Such an outright declaration makes me sick to my stomach.

"What's the commotion?" The razor-nailed hairdresser stomps toward our group, eyes flashing an angry red. "Get back to work, our VIP guest will be coming any minute. He specifically requested that chandelier for his session. And, you two"—she bows to Dura and Raisal—"I'm afraid the parlor will be closing soon for our VIP guest's arrival. Could you clear out soon? I recommend heading to the diner for a refreshing snack."

I scoff. I can't believe my eyes.... She's really treating these kiddy jinn like a pair of nobles. She sweeps away, joining the other workers who scurry around like a hive of bees. They sweep up locks of hair and organize every lotion bottle by color.

Only a few seconds pass before our war strikes up again. Sughal shakes his head, claw fingernails digging into his scalp. "Do you think we have another option?" he says to me. "If we don't trick humans...it's a life of labor for *us*. My maa borrowed money from the owner a century ago, and our family is still trying to pay back that debt."

The yellow jinn pipes up too. "Dura used to actually be a patron. But I heard her baba got on the wrong side of the owner and she got sent to the working quarters."

Dura's head hangs low after that statement, and I'm equally as shocked. Every single one of these jinn children have undergone tragedy or swindling, and now they're paying the price. But this *shouldn't* have happened. As much as I despise these fire-twirling demons, I see myself in them. I see all the mica mining children in them.

"It should already be hanging!" comes a familiar, whiny voice.

"We're deeply sorry, please forgive us. The children are newly hired—"

"Enough! You haven't even cleared the place out yet!"

I turn to find the source of the commotion, but my stomach instantly drops like the swoop of a bird. Adorned in a fluffy pink robe, red hair falling across his back like bloody waves, one of his pearly horns chopped off—it's the Painted Boy, Mirza. *He's* the VIP guest? Now the wild demands make more sense.

The parlor staff hush down into a flurry of whispers, but when I see them pointing our way, I feel a zing through my bones: it's fight or flight time.

The Painted Boy scowls as he struts toward us, arms crossed and stare penetrating. He's a foot taller, but he doesn't seem nearly as intimidating when one of his horns looks like a carrot someone took a bite out of.

The jinn children immediately bow their heads in a display of obedience, as if Mirza's every wish and whim can decide their fate. But considering the hotel we're in, that assumption might not be far off. . . .

Mirza strolls straight up to Sughal, leaning down until they're only an inch apart. "Are you blind, fur-boy? Or are you willfully ignoring the fact that you all are the only ones left in this parlor during *my private session?*"

If Sughal stares at Mirza's chopped-off horn for a second

longer, I'm afraid Mirza might have the same happen to Sughal's horn. "S-sorry, sir." He averts his gaze and swallows. "We came to set up the chandelier you requested."

Mirza taps his chin. "That's right, I wanted a shower of starlight above me. Yet I don't see a single sparkle."

"Right away, sir! Forgive us." Sughal signals to his yellow friend, and they dart away to find a ladder.

Mirza straightens, deciding on his next victim. Aroofa and Tahir are shaking, Faisal's eyes bulge as if he's looking at a talking sculpture, and then there's me—a girl whose patience is thinning with each ticking second, about to rip my hair off because *time is running out and I still don't know how to escape this wretched hotel.*

"Pesky humans, am I right?" Raisal snickers.

Mirza pays no heed. He lifts one perfectly arched brow. "Why haven't you left yet?"

Dura makes a move to grab Raisal's arm, but he brushes her off. "I'm just waiting for this face mask to dry. It shouldn't take more than a minute."

Mirza hums at that, lips broadening into a morbid, glittery smile. He turns to face us, and just from the way he glances at me with his bloody eyes, I know something horrible is about to happen.

"Let me wash it off for you." He flicks his wrist, calling over a parlor worker with a bowl of water in his hands.

Mirza grabs the bowl and slowly pours it over Raisal's head. My breath catches.

I should be laughing. After all the deceitful moments I've shared with Raisal, it's only natural for laughter to burst from my gut. But something else is bubbling in there instead—dread, the slow realization that nothing is as I thought it was.

"Not only have you refused orders, but you've also mocked my authority," Mirza says, glass shattering as he smashes the empty bowl against the floor. "Just because you tricked your human, you think you're immune now? Deserving of a medal? A plaque in our hall of fame? You aren't any better than those human children over there— heck, you're probably more tragic."

Raisal's face drops, eyes widening. I recognize that face. I've seen it on so many other children, and even more on myself. The face when you finally understand the truth— that contractors don't want the best for you, that you're just one discardable worker, and that the freedom you thought you possessed . . . is all a sham.

Raisal sinks to the ground, and just like that, he's back to working, picking up the glass shards as they prick his fingers and draw blood. "Please, don't take away my patronage. I'm sorry—"

"Pitiful," Mirza says. "I forget how naive some of you

can be. Allow me to enlighten you. Why do you think the hotel allows jinn to trick humans into working?" He cocks his head, looking at Tahir.

Tahir stumbles back from the weight of Mirza's stare, stammering out, "Um, because jinn love to swindle?"

"Not wrong. But not entirely correct." Mirza hums. He turns to Faisal. "How about you?"

Faisal fidgets with the hem of his kurta. "Because j-jinn and humans have never liked each other?"

Mirza shakes his head, finally facing me, chin high as he awaits my answer. "What do you think?"

It's worse than I thought. The glitter and sparkle of the Sijj Palace is just a curtain to what it hides behind: exploitation. Dura, Raisal, all the other jinn children with high hopes of living in luxury, they're just this realm's version of the contractors... exploiting others so they themselves can avoid being exploited. It's a vicious cycle with no end in sight. The poor stay poor because the rich aren't willing to spread their resources.

My tongue is as rough as sandpaper, throat almost too tight to let the words free. "You let jinn children trick humans, reward them with patronage, only to trick them back into working too. So it'll double the labor power."

Mirza claps. "Ding. Ding. Ding."

Raisal's jaw hangs, his bloody fingers twitching against

the glass shards. Dura's chest rises and falls in shallow breaths. Us poor children usually never have "reality checks" because our reality just happens to be that way— straightforward, with no room for imagination. But when we do get a slap back to reality, it's like having our hearts ripped out of our chests, stumbling through a dark tunnel with no light at the end.

Mirza leans down to face Raisal. "What are you doing? Get back to work."

And so the vicious cycle continues. I feel hollow, all hope and inkling of determination lost. If every part of this hotel is a deception, who says us humans really have a chance to escape? We might be from a different realm, but our fate here is the same—this is no fairy tale, no backyard adventure. It's just one of thousands of exploitation schemes.

"How many times do I have to say it? Everyone, *leave*!" Mirza yells, his fiery hair whipping into the air.

I stagger back with the rest of the children, hastily heading over to the glass door of the parlor.

"Except you."

The hairs on the back of my neck stand. I turn slowly, and to my greatest dread, Mirza is pointing at me.

"Let me reward you for getting that question right."

CHAPTER 18

Betrayal or Betrothal

I'd be knocking on death's door if I refused Mirza's demand, so I sneak one last glance at Faisal before forcing my heavy feet back toward the Painted Boy. He struts behind a curtain into his VIP suite, decorated with pink cushions and pinker rugs. The parlor workers follow as well, offering Mirza platters of sweets as they recite the evening's itinerary. I roll my eyes when I hear "painting nails" and "foot scrub," followed by "hair mask."

My veins are thrumming the same way they do when I scour the mines, but there's a different rush to it...fear instead of adrenaline. The air in this parlor is heavy with unease, so I do my best to disperse it.

"What are you getting so dolled up for? Is there someone you're trying to impress?" I wiggle my brows, trying to wipe off his scowl with a few lighthearted jokes. If Raisal's got him worked up, I don't want to be on the receiving end of that fury.

I thought it was just the pigment on Mirza's cheeks at first, but when I stare for a moment longer, I realize he's actually *blushing*. I lick my lips, an engine for teasing suddenly roaring to life inside me. Just when I'm about to shift gears into full throttle, he clogs my pipes entirely.

"Don't talk to me about beauty when you clearly know so little about it. I mean"—he eyes me up and down as his lips stretch into a scowl—"just look at you." Mirza juts out his chin and walks past me.

Now, there's a fine line between teasing and being outright offensive. I don't recall ever flinging words at him that burned when they landed, and that's how I feel right now: roasted.

"Is there any other reason you brought me here besides wanting a human punching bag?" I sneer.

Mirza sighs, clicking his tongue like I'm some dog he's been ordered to watch. "Not just ugly but stupid too? I didn't ask you to speak."

Heat boils in my gut. I've been plenty polite, keeping my comments within the realm of banter, but I'm not afraid to get real with this spoiled brat. After seeing Raisal's entire world flip upside down and all his hopes crushed in a matter of seconds, I've figured out the way the Sijj Palace works. There's no going up for me now.

"Are you having this spa session because you're ashamed? Are you afraid someone else will take your place for the prettiest, most annoying brat just because I chopped off your horn?"

Mirza's hazel eyes narrow at me from his perch on a lounge chair. "Out."

I roll my eyes and get ready to take my leave. Fine. If he won't play my games, then I'm not going to waste my time trying.

"Not you," Mirza snaps. "I meant the parlor staff."

The nail artist, who's carrying an entire tray of polish, turns 180 degrees and steps back out the door. The jinn carrying platters of food cough uncomfortably before filing out as well. One by one, the staff of the parlor bow to Mirza before disappearing behind a curtain and out of his private suite.

Mirza lets out a little *humph* and turns all his attention to me. The way he's sitting on that lounge chair makes him look like a ruler on a throne.

"Since you don't seem to be nearly as grateful as you should be, I'll spell this out for you." He takes a sip of his chai and sets the cup down. "A jinn only cuts their horns for two reasons. The first reason is outdated, nobody follows such a tradition anymore, but when jinn soldiers got promoted in the army, they used to cut off one of their horns and offer it to the general that trained them. The other reason..." Mirza whispers and looks away from me, his cheeks flushing from pink to red. "In some jinn cultures, lovers would cut off each other's horn and keep it as a promise of...betrothal."

It sounds like cutting off a horn is quite the serious display. Fine, I was in the wrong. But it was an *accident*. I scratch my head and raise a brow. Now, betrothal? What does that word even mean? I shrug. "So what?"

Mirza springs to his feet in a flash. His hair sprawls out around him like a furiously whipping cape. "So you took away my chance at a love life!"

"Huh?"

Tears threaten to spill from his eyes. I'm just about to call him out for being an overdramatic imp when he slaps down his ultimate card.

"Take responsibility for your actions. Marry me."

There's only so much ridiculousness I can take in one day. I pinch my arm. If this is all just a nightmare and I wake up in the working quarters for another tiring day, it'll still make more sense than this.

"Have you completely lost it?" I shout. "Was your brain inside your horn?"

Mirza stomps toward me. "What you did cost me all my hopes for a romance. Now when someone looks at me, they think I'm going to be married!" he huffs, pulling at his hair. "My father didn't want to arrange anything since you're a human, but I can't take this humiliation any longer. You must marry me!"

A sudden memory rouses a wave of goose bumps over my skin. I recall the jinn couple at the banquet exchanging horns. They were getting married....

"Nope. One thousand times no. Never going to happen." My face is set in a straight line. If this is a joke, I need to let him know that at least I'm serious about my answer. "I don't even think that's possible—"

"It is. Jinn and humans have been together before. It's rare, but we can make this work, Nora."

"It's *Nura*."

Mirza grabs both of my hands and pulls me close until I can see his perfectly flawless skin and the glaze of gloss shining on his lips. "I can give you anything you want. Sweets, clothes, servants. You name it, I'll give it. But first, we should start with a makeover—"

I swat my hands away from him, eyes wide. He's actually serious about this. "If you're such a hopeless romantic, you're never going to be happy with me." I'm trying to make him see straight.

"I wanted to believe in love. I've waited centuries for the right person to sweep me off my feet, but look at what fate decided for me. *You*," he whines, pulling at his long red locks. "My parents fought enough times to stamp out my idea of love, but still I hoped for something true. Now I know better than to try to seek something that doesn't exist. If you're my only option, I'll settle."

My mouth opens and closes, but no words that I can use to tackle this outrageous announcement come to mind.

"Nura, you're smarter than the others. In the human realm, do you think it'll be any different? You'll still be exploited by people who never want to see you rise and succeed. You're only going to live a life of misery in the human realm, and here as well if you refuse my proposal. Get married to me, and your problems go away."

It's true that Mirza can get anything he wants at his every beck and call. A comfortable life of luxury with no worries about what I'll eat for dinner—it sounds like a dream. Draped in silks, lying on a plush bed, getting dolled up so I can look my best...I experienced all those firsts here in this hotel, and now Mirza's offering me that and more.

Mirza steps closer to me, and this time I don't back away. "There's no need to be worried. Or guilty that your family back home will never have the kind of riches you'll get with me." He brushes a strand of hair from my face. "Once the hotel's binding magic is sealed, you'll forget them anyway. You'll be entirely free."

It's a low punch straight to my gut, but I can almost admire how twisted this situation is. My family is the only reason I work. I hate having to see Maa's back hunched deeper than the day before. I hate the cold sweats I get when Adeel asks me if there's anything he can do to help. And I'd hate myself even more if I never made enough money to send Kinza and Rabia to school so that at least the two of them can climb out of this vicious cycle.

A dry chuckle escapes my lips. Mirza's not only offering me all the luxury I can imagine but a foolproof way to never feel guilty about any of it. It's what the monster inside me craves, and right now, it's practically clawing to get out and shake Mirza's hand on my behalf. I sigh, pressing my lips into a tight line.

"I see." Mirza hums, gaze sliding around the room as he sets a hand to his hip. "You're worried about your human friends. I can settle something for them, small benefits like shorter workdays and better food. Tell me, Nura, what do you say?"

It's corrupt, wicked on multiple levels, and has my gut spiraling into sickness. "I—"

"Say no!"

I spin around to see Faisal sprawled across the floor, limbs tangled in the curtain that's separating the private suite from the rest of the parlor. Jinn in peacoats are trying to pull him back, but he squirms out of their grasps, crawling forward to stand next to me. Was he eavesdropping this entire time?

Mirza's eyes narrow. "This doesn't concern you."

"It d-does. She's my friend."

"She *started* this!" Mirza yells, shoving Faisal so hard he tumbles aside and lands on his back. "If she hadn't cut my horn, I wouldn't have to stoop so low in the first place!"

"Faisal!" I gasp. I crouch down and lift Faisal into my arms, checking to see if he's hurt.

Mirza pauses his outrage to stare at us for a moment. He waves the parlor workers out of the suite as a smirk snaps onto his face. "So he's the reason why? You like that pathetic boy so much you refuse to marry me?"

Anything but this. I'm not afraid to yell Mirza's ears off if it means I'm the only one thrown in a dungeon. But Faisal's here now. Any wrong move or mistake in my words, and both of us could end up on the side of Mirza's wrath. How do I protect him? Mirza wants me, and if Faisal's in the way, I can't see this ending well.

"Mirza…," I begin. But before I can even think of a counter, Faisal jumps to his feet.

"I'm not pathetic," Faisal snaps. His arms are trembling, but his brows are furrowed, and his chest square with determination. It's the first time I've seen Faisal truly angry. He turns his head around to look at me, gaze burning so bright it could light this entire hotel on fire. "And I'm *not* a coward."

Then he's back to facing Mirza, arms crossed, chin up and unrelenting. His voice no longer shakes, and there's no more hesitation before he utters a word. He used to consider if it was worth it to speak, to have his stutter on display. But I can see the change in his eyes—if his words come out stuttering, he doesn't give a care in the world.

"Respect h-her wishes," Faisal says, fists clenched. "You have another horn. That gives you another chance."

"Another chance?" Mirza exclaims, arms flailing. "With my botched horns, I'm no longer considered beautiful. How will I find love like this? You don't understand!" He faces me, hands balled into fists. "Say yes."

Fear kept my feet glued inside this suite as I listened to Mirza's every word. It stoked the fire in my gut, the hunger of the monster inside me, but I'm past that now. If Faisal can burst through the doors with more confidence than I've seen in all his years combined, I can't let him outshine me.

"No." I swallow. "Never."

If the world has abandoned my family and so many other poor ones like it, then we only have each other. My siblings rely on me. Maa, although she hates to admit it, needs me. People in power love to pit the helpless against each other—it's an easy way to keep them busy and weak so that they'll never rise high enough to fight. It feels so natural, almost instinctual to follow, that my brain is practically screaming at me to stop being foolish and just accept the proposal.

But I don't want to play into this vicious cycle. If the world is just a thousand layers of frauds and schemes, then the only way I can be proud of myself is if I'm not on the side that swindles. There will be more children like me, tumbling into the warm embrace of the Sijj Palace, only to be tricked into a life of servitude. And if Mirza thinks I can sit next to him and laugh while it happens, he's absolutely wrong.

Mirza grunts as he lunges forward and grabs Faisal's face. Faisal yelps and squirms in his grasp, but I've seen what happens when the Painted Boy shows his true colors. I remember the way his eyes turned bloody, and I can't let him quench his bloodthirst on my best friend.

"Faisal!"

Mirza squeezes harder, his smile turning wicked as he presses his forehead against Faisal's. My heart drops when Faisal screams, eyes rolling back into his head.

"Stop! What are you doing?" I yell.

But then they both drop to the floor like slabs of meat, unconscious. I pounce over to Faisal. His eyes are closed, lips slightly parted, but he's still breathing—even if it's as light as the brush of a feather. "Faisal?"

Faisal's eyes open slowly. I gasp. The whites of his eyes are red.

CHAPTER 19

When Earth Meets Fire

Didn't your parents tell you the stories?" Faisal's lips melt into a smirk. "That you shouldn't play with jinn?"

I crawl backward, jaw hanging. "No... please."

The real Faisal is no longer with me. Why didn't I expect this? I've heard stories of jinn possessing humans, but Maa always told me it was the product of kala jadu—that a human has to call upon a jinn to curse someone else into being haunted. But I've been too naive. This isn't the realm of humans. This is where the laws of jinn thrive.

"What'll you do now? The poor boy is hurting. I'm sure

to him it must feel like his insides are on fire," Mirza speaks through Faisal's body.

My hands are tingling with the urge to punch Mirza to hell and back, but he's in Faisal's body. How am I supposed to react? How do I get him out of there? Beads of sweat roll down my neck. My breaths are raggedy. When I look at the twisted expression that's plastered on my best friend's face, there's nothing more that I want than to stop this.

"Mirza, please. Let him go."

"Not until you agree to marry me."

"Stop being ridiculous!"

Mirza clicks his tongue. "Would you rather spend eternity working for this hotel? Or spend it with me in luxury? *You're* being ridiculous."

The monster inside me growls, hungry to accept. Usually, I do well to satisfy it, but this time I can't. The best choice isn't to feed that hungry monster everything I can, but to quell it and, like the Craftsman said, suppress its chaos.

Mirza wants things just for the sake of wanting them. I used to think that would be my greatest goal in life, to reach a point where it no longer mattered what I bought, or how much it cost, or what it was even used for. As long as I wanted it—I could get it. But watching Mirza now, taking over Faisal's body, I scowl. When you reach a certain level of wealth, everything that comes after is just dirty money.

I'm starting to recognize what *true greed* is. I used to beat myself up over indulging in gulab jamuns, eating more than my share of rice, or spending too much time in Meerabagh's market with twitchy fingers. But I scoff. My greed, the other children's greed, is practically a joke. We want food, clothes, things necessary to our survival, and yet powerful people prey on that fact and use it to trap us. *That's* what true greed is, what Mirza has, what the owner has…when you keep on wanting things until you forget why you wanted them in the first place. I'd never forgive myself if that's where my greed led.

I drop to my knees and roll sideways, swerving around Faisal and grabbing Mirza's limp body. Now that Mirza's soul is prancing around in Faisal's body, he can no longer defend his own. I grab scissors from a table and point the blade at the long expanse of Mirza's throat.

Mirza, in Faisal's body, springs toward me, arms outstretched. I clench the scissors harder. "Let him go, and I won't hurt you."

"So you've made your decision."

I press the blade against Mirza's skin. I'm done making shapeless threats. Faisal's still in there, probably screaming for help, writhing in pain. I'm no longer feeling polite.

"Do it. I don't care," Mirza says, a smirk lighting his face. "You underestimate us jinn once again. We don't bleed like humans do. Cut me up if you'd like. It won't kill me."

I grit my teeth. My thoughts travel back to the Craftsman and his wisdom about jinn and their childish desires. But what if a jinn is so childish that they don't listen to even an ounce of reason?

But then I remember children also love to bluff.

I hover the scissors over Mirza's face instead of his neck. "You may not bleed, but you won't be pretty anymore. Or should I cut off your other horn too?"

Instantly his face drops, eyes wide. His brows tilt upward, and he falls to the ground, kneeling in front of me. "Don't you dare..."

I can't help the smirk that melts onto my face. If he's going to bluff, so will I. I know where the Painted Boy's priorities are. He *is* the figurehead of this hotel. If he loses his looks, he loses his reputation and fame. It's game over.

"Let Faisal go." I steady the scissors at a dangerous angle to his cheek.

"Okay! I'll leave his body," Mirza wheezes, hands up. "Just please don't hurt my face."

And then Faisal's eyes roll back into his head once again, body glowing with a pink aura. He convulses once, twice, and then hits the floor with a thud.

I spring toward him, brushing the dark tangle of curls from his sweating face. His eyes are moving from under his eyelids and there's a furrow to his brows, but he's not waking up. "Faisal," I shout. This is taking too long. I slap him.

"Gah!" he yelps, jerking awake.

Then I squeeze him into a hug.

I could probably stay in this position forever if it wasn't for the heavy panting and wheezing that begin to fill the parlor suite. I glance around and see Mirza back in his body, but he's crawling sluggishly, tongue hanging as his sweaty robe clings to him. Long strands of red hair fall askew over his face, and the gaunt hollows of his cheeks look even deeper. Mirza is in worse shape than the old grandpas selling figs in Meerabagh's market.

Faisal's voice is hoarse, like he swallowed liquid fire, but it's confident. "Did possessing me suck away all your energy?"

"I—I can't believe you...," Mirza wheezes. "Tried to take all I have left."

I scoff as I get to my feet, pulling Faisal up as well. "Oh, stop being such a drama queen. You're the owner's son. You have more than most can even imagine."

"But if I didn't have a face like this," Mirza sobs, grazing his cheeks as if they'd disintegrate at any moment, "my father would never let me have my way. I'm just a pawn in his schemes. Every time the hotel needs more sponsorships, or we get another VIP guest, he shows me off like some kind of sparkly medal. I must look beautiful. It's the only reason he treats me well. If I didn't spend every moment taking care of myself...I might end up like my uncle." Mirza wipes the snot from his nose across his fluffy sleeve. "Since my father became the sole owner of the Sijj Palace, it's never been the same around here."

"You dad wasn't always the sole owner? Then who else was there?"

"My father's brother, the Demiurge. They opened this hotel together."

"Brother?" I pounce forward, grabbing the collar of Mirza's robe. "Where's the Demiurge? He didn't really leave on some work trip forever, did he?"

Mirza gasps and clamps a hand over his mouth. His words are muffled, but my ears are so alert right now I hear him as clear as glass: "I've already said too much."

Once again the scissors are in my hand, and from the way Mirza looks, he doesn't have the power to stop me. I wouldn't really disfigure his face, he's so annoyingly theatrical about it, but it's still my best threat.

"It's just—the Demiurge, well..." Mirza's chest rises and falls, labored from the stress of speaking. He looks everywhere but at me, and when he says the next few words, I understand why. "He's...he's actually here. He's the Craftsman."

CHAPTER 20

As Being Is to Becoming, So Is Truth to Belief

I don't wait.

Once Mirza utters the words *He's the Craftsman*, two seconds barely pass before I'm sprinting out of the parlor and down into the working quarters with Faisal in tow. I slam the wooden door open, shove past other jinn and human children, and stop outside the welding room. The sign on the door is turned so the IN USE label is toward me. He's in there. I knock with three hard raps.

Footsteps echo before the door glides open and the shadow of the towering Craftsman hovers over me. He's wearing his usual baggy suit and heavy-duty apron, complete with the strange beaked mask.

"Hello, children," he says. "Did Mirza like the chandelier?"

I scowl. "Your nephew's a brat, you know that?"

The Craftsman freezes, and his grip on the doorknob tightens. I can't see his expression behind the mask, but his mirrored goggles reflect my face, so if he's staring at me, my frown shows I'm done playing games.

"We know, sir. You're the Demiurge," Faisal says. His voice is quiet, words like finger taps instead of hammer strikes, as if to avoid breaking the Craftsman's brittle feelings.

Unlike Faisal, I'm burning. We've been running around on the verge of insanity trying to look for the Demiurge, and yet he was standing in front of us this entire time. If he had any decency, any fondness for us like he claims he does, he would've *told* us how to escape this hotel. I could've been eaten alive by Shahmaran, Faisal could've been scorched by the owner, and heck, I might've been married to Mirza.

"Why didn't you tell us?" I shout. The surrounding kids snap their gazes toward us, some even ready to throw fists as I confront the Craftsman, our supposed *leader*.

He sighs. "Come."

The Craftsman walks back into the welding room. We follow, passing by welding sticks and rolls of steel wire. There's a soldering station in the corner and an exhaust pipe hanging from above, but when we near the back of the room, the Craftsman taps the brick wall in a sequence, and I realize it's not just a welding chamber.

The back wall starts moving like a puzzle, bricks rearranging until a gap forms, darkness shrouding what lies ahead. The Craftsman walks into the gap, and instantly the darkness swallows him.

I glance at Faisal. He bites his lip. We nod at the same time—and step through.

My jaw hangs. Past the darkness and uncertainty is a small study. There are papers everywhere—pasted over the walls, flung across the floor, dangling at the edges of the wooden desk. Some are even clipped on strings and hanging from the ceiling like forgotten laundry.

I tiptoe around candle pots that are more pools of wax than they are sticks, and I grab one off the floor and direct its light to get a better look at the documents. I raise my brows. They're blueprints for different machines—everything from toys to giant, complex gadgets that can capture and store sunlight to use at night.

"Are you impressed?" the Craftsman asks. His voice is amused, but there's a certain tinge to it, as if it drips with somberness instead of mischief. "These are the kinds of things I craft. Just tinkering objects. Mere toys. If I am the Demiurge, do you think I'd be wasting my time on such petty things?"

I cross my arms. "You *were* the Demiurge. But you got demoted. And now you're the Craftsman."

Faisal elbows my arm, eyes wide, as if to say, *That's rude!*

But I don't want to swindle my way around words like the Craftsman has been doing. Ever since I first met him, he's talked in twists, like his sentences are walls in a maze, and I have to search for the way out myself.

But I want honesty.

My blunt and straightforward words seem to have struck a chord with the Craftsman. He glances at me, then to the floor, and then to the wall of blueprints that stare back at us like a very personal diary containing his every secret. And I'm about to uncover them all.

"Demoted?" He chuckles dryly. "That's certainly one way to put it."

The floor screeches as the Craftsman pulls the chair out from under the desk. He flops onto it, head in his hands. But then his fingers curl behind his neck, flicking off the straps of his mask, and I hold my breath.

His long blue hair waltzes over his shoulders first. Then beads of sweat roll down his face—the same face I saw in the owner's office. The jinn who had his arm around the owner, smiling widely, shark teeth shining and red eyes sparkling, is right in front of me. His face looks familiar, one that's more warmth than fire.

"I hide behind this mask so no one will recognize that I'm the Demiurge. I don't want to give the children false hope," the Craftsman whispers. "Because I don't know how to escape this hotel either."

"B-but," Faisal counters, "you're the Demiurge. You built the Sijj Palace yourself."

The Craftsman sighs. "I'm no longer who you think I am. The Demiurge? Only the idea of him remains. The same goes for the hotel I've built.... There's been too many changes since I've last been aboveground."

I didn't barrel down the stairs to see the Craftsman sulking. I want answers, not surrender. "You're the founder of this hotel. Why are you stuck in these dingy working quarters?"

The Craftsman slides open a drawer and pulls out five rolls of battered, aged blueprints. When he unravels them along the desk, Faisal and I peer closer. My heart freezes.

"These are the original blueprints for the Sijj Palace." The Craftsman brushes his fingers across the sketch marks, outlining each section. "This is the courtyard—it turned out a lot bigger than I initially designed. This is the banquet hall.

I made sure the chandeliers set the mood nicely. And this…"
His voice lowers to a whisper, unsteady, like a river that's
thinned out into just a trickle of water. "This was supposed
to be a daycare for children, but the idea was scrapped."

"Why?" I ask.

The Craftsman rests his cheek against his hand, red eyes
twinkling as he gazes across the room. "My brother wanted
to run this hotel differently. When we opened, the Sijj Palace was quite successful. We had offers for sponsorships and
VIP guests from all over who wanted to stay here. But they
wanted us to remodel rooms, to build new wings, and we
didn't have the power available—our magic is finite. So my
brother suggested we employ children. I refused. And the
VIP guests—some of them were criminals, offering hefty
sums if we let them stay. But I declined again. My brother
and I…we butted heads whenever it came to money."

The Craftsman shakes his head, long blue hair twirling
like waves across his shoulders. "Money: how to spend it,
how to make more of it. My brother said I wasn't fit to be a
businessman. That I was foolish. That I'd lost my intellect.
That I should hand over the hotel to him and stay out of it."

Faisal's brows are tilted with sorrow. "That's horrible.
How could he say that to his own b-brother?"

"I wish I could've handled his hatred differently," the
Craftsman whispers.

"What did he hate so much for him to become so cruel?" I snap.

"Himself." The Craftsman sighs. "We started off poor, and in a world that lifts up the rich and kicks the poor even lower, it was a miracle we even got as far as building the hotel. For years people told us it was impossible. But no matter how much my brother hated everyone who belittled us, he hated himself the most."

The Craftsman's glimmering gaze wanders over his old blueprints, and I wonder if he sees something that I can't. "He hated our origins—pitiful, poor...and thought the only way to remove those titles was to bring the Sijj Palace to a level of success where no one could question us. It didn't matter what that took.

"That's why I refused him," the Craftsman says. "So my brother decided to get rid of me. But the funniest part of this whole story"—the Craftsman chuckles, shaking his head—"is that a part of my soul is tied to all my creations. He couldn't separate me from this hotel, so he tricked even his own family, trapping me in the working quarters forever. Where no one from outside could see me and I could no longer see outside."

I swallow. It brings me back to our conversation the other day, when the Craftsman asked me how it felt to taste the air and feel the dirt beneath my feet. How long has he been cursed to stay in these dingy quarters? An eternity? I'm utterly confused. If the Craftsman and his brother were being thrown money from the day the hotel opened, why did their lives get harder instead of easier?

I think back to my own family. Maa, me, and my three siblings, sharing our two-room hut. I always think that if I could gain one more rupee, we would be so much happier. No more day-old rice and curry. No more mining. Just a tight-knit family with ambitious goals and more money than we know what to do with.

But that's not the case, is it?

"Why did you create the hotel in the first place, if money wasn't your goal?" I ask, the words wavering like a boat coasting on a stormy sea. I've always known money to be the final goal of everything in life. When I saw children in their white uniforms hobbling over to Mccrabagh's school, I didn't bother teasing them about having to stay inside with a book all day. Because education meant getting a good job, and a good job meant good money. When I worked in the mines, no one even questioned it—the answer was obvious. If someone were to ask any of the kids why they hopped into the tunnels and dug until their fingers bled, we'd all have the same response: money.

"Order," the Craftsman says, gaze locking onto mine. "This world is disorderly chaos. The more that people wander across the world, the greater the chance they can lose themselves. Obstacles, pain, loss—it all changes a person. That's why I created the Sijj Palace, as a place where people can restore their souls to a state of intellect, and calm their chaotic edges through relaxation. It's connected through portals so that jinn from all over the world can become guests. A multidimensional hotel that closes its doors to no one."

There's a shine to the Craftsman's red eyes, as if he's trying to suck back the tears that threaten to fall. "But now, the Sijj Palace has become a place where qareens are kidnapping their human counterparts, children are being used to do the dirty work, and I'm trapped in a cage forever. As much as I tried to eliminate chaos, this hotel has fallen to it."

I scoff. "Laws are flimsy when there are people who don't understand why they've been made in the first place."

Education. I know I'm smart, but now I'm thinking... how much smarter could I be? How clever can my schemes get? Perhaps the pencils those schoolgirls carry really do hold a power I'm not yet aware of.

"Exactly." The Craftsman smiles, as if I've finally found my way out of his maze of words. "There is the wealth of money, but even greater is the wealth of mind. People will descend back into disorder if they don't hone their wits.

If they lack the education. Ever since the aim of the hotel became making more and more money, it's all my brother lives for. He threw away his morals for money. He deserted me for money. If I had the chance to go back, I would never build this hotel. I've tried every plan of escape I could, but nothing worked. That's why when you told me you were going to find the secret to escaping...I truly hoped you would. Because maybe it meant I could escape as well."

My legs are trembling, knees too weak to hold my body straight. I drift to the floor, head clutched in my hands as I process the Craftsman's words. He's locked in this hotel just like we are. He doesn't know the secret to escaping, even if he is the Demiurge. Tonight, as midnight strikes, when Eid al-Adha is officially over, we'll have no way out. I'll never be able to see my family again. When I think of my baba and what little I remember of him, a shiver runs down my back. If I'm gone forever, what will my family remember of me? Will Maa just think I was an annoying brat that never listened to her? Will Adeel only recall the way I teased him and pulled at his ears? Will Kinza and Rabia even remember my face?

I can't accept that.

"You're telling us...that we're stuck here?" Faisal sucks back a hiccup, and his head droops to hide the well of tears in his eyes.

I pace back and forth in the room. The blueprints plastered all over become a dizzying background of black and white. I run my hands through my hair, clutch my chin, and scratch my head. I've never been book smart. I can't read well like Faisal, and I can't build the things the Craftsman can either. But I've almost always been able to get myself out of impossible situations, even if I have to bring the walls down around me to get there.

Maybe that's it—maybe escaping this enchanted hotel really is impossible. Unless the hotel *no longer exists*.

"Let's destroy the Sijj Palace."

CHAPTER 21

It Was, It Is, It Shall Be

Faisal's head whips toward me, and the Craftsman stops breathing. They stare at me with wide, trembling eyes like I've just dug a hole in their chests and ripped out their hearts.

"If the hotel is in ruins, we're no longer bound to the magic that belongs to it. We'll be free."

The Craftsman anchors an arm on his chair as he gets to his feet. He glides toward me, face frozen in an incredulous expression. Then his palms wrap around both of my cheeks, squishing them like a sandwich. I can't tell if he's angry with me for daring to suggest destroying his very own creation, but I won't take back my words. I meant what I said.

"You genius kids," the Craftsman whispers.

My eyes widen. That's a word I rarely ever hear in Meerabagh, and definitely never applied to me.

He twirls around, hands clasped to his head, breaking into a fit of laughter. Then all of a sudden, he squeezes Faisal into a hug and grabs my waist to throw me into the air.

"It can work. It can finally work. At first, I never wanted to destroy the Sijj Palace. It is still my greatest creation. But it's done so much more harm than good."

"How do we do it?" I gasp. I finally feel air filling my lungs—filling them with hope.

"Destroying it might be possible from the inside out, but there's a problem—making sure everyone within it remains safe from harm." He drums his fingers against the desk. "There has to be a way. . . ."

"The portals!" Faisal jumps to his feet. "M-maybe we can destroy the Sijj Palace but still keep everyone safe? There m-must be some way the portals can help us. Each of the wards has special qualities. We just need to figure out how to use that to our advantage."

The Craftsman's lips fall open until they stretch into a wide grin. "You're right, Faisal. It's all coming together now. We need to plant a bomb."

"Bomb?" I can't imagine how that's going to keep any-one safe.

"The reason I couldn't do it myself is because I didn't want to destroy the palace with all its patrons still inside. But there's a way around that." The Craftsman pulls out more blueprints of the Sijj Palace. "Just like Faisal said, this is where the portals come into play. You likely know that the hotel has three wards: Space, Matter, and Time. In some ways they are connected, and in others they are not. The Matter ward is special—things happening outside don't affect it, as long as time has stopped. If you send every patron through the portals and into the Matter ward, stop time using the Time ward, and plant a bomb in the Space ward, the Palace will collapse—but the patrons will remain unhurt."

"I…" I scratch my head. "You're going to have to repeat that."

The Craftsman chuckles, tousling my dark curls. He's too ecstatic to be annoyed with our confusion. For the first time it's as if the candle of the Craftsman's soul has been lit. "Here's the plan. The working quarters are in the Time ward, where we are currently. I can fiddle with the switches here to make time stop in the Matter ward, but it'll only last sixty seconds. I know it's not a lot of time, but I only built it in as a safety measure. If we can plant a bomb in the

Space ward while time is frozen in the Matter ward, nothing in the Matter ward will be affected."

I remember the way the carpets rippled in the hallways of the Matter ward. How the noise and commotion of the hotel couldn't be heard from inside. Nothing was as it seemed or was affected in the way things usually were. Maybe that entire section of the palace exists somewhere else, between dimensions, in a place where the normal laws of science don't apply.

I nod, a smile snapping onto my face. "Got it. We gather everyone in the Matter ward so they'll stay out of harm's way, and set off a bomb in the Space ward while time is frozen for sixty seconds. When the bomb goes off—the Sijj Palace will be destroyed."

"That's right."

"When's the earliest you can make the bomb?" I ask.

The Craftsman bites his lip as he pulls out more papers and pencils. He skims over inventory documents to check what tools he has in store, then flicks his gaze to me. My heart drops. I've seen that look one too many times: from Faisal when he's worried about me digging too deep in the mines, when Maa pats my head and says she wishes she could buy me gulab jamuns every day, and now I see it here again—from the Craftsman.

"What is it?" I snap.

"The earliest I could finish it is...tomorrow."

I swallow. That's past the deadline. We'll be tied to the hotel forever, memory wiped before we even get a chance to plant it.

"Let us help," I say suddenly. "Why make it yourself when there's all these kids off the clock?"

I think of Maa, how she refuses to let me spend another day mica mining. I think of myself too, and the plea in Adeel's eyes as he silently begs me to admit how tired I am at the end of the day—and the start. And when I see the Craftsman, his brows slowly rising, it's on his face too: that self-reliance we've all built up to get through the day. But we don't need to go through it alone.

"If we make it together," I say with a smile, "escaping won't have to stay just an *idea*."

The Craftsman drums his fingers against the desk, brows still threaded with worry. I've only untangled one of his concerns. "It is possible...but who is going to plant it?"

I rake a hand through my hair, laughter bubbling from my chest and bursting out my mouth. "That's it? You haven't seen how fast I move in the mines. In a few hours I can collect baskets upon baskets of mica. This'll be *nothing*."

Faisal glances at me. His lips burn red from being bitten too hard, but they finally stretch into a smile. "She's right.

And I'm quick at sifting mica from dirt. I'll collect every patron in no time."

The Craftsman looks from Faisal to me, his brows turned upside down. His mouth is pressed into a tight line, as if he's trying to hold back a slew of warnings, like an overprotective father that doesn't want his children to be out traversing the world.

But all he says is this: "My brother will come after you when he realizes I've stopped time. This plan is dangerous. Are you still willing to do it?"

I smirk. It sounds a little confusing and twisted, and there's a lot of room for this plan to go wrong, but if it's our ticket out of here, then I'll do what I've done my entire life—risk it.

"It'll be Tuesday soon, won't it?" I ask. "Mr. Waleed sells gulab jamun on Tuesdays. So if I don't destroy the Sijj Palace in time and get my hands on a gulab, I'm never going to forgive myself."

CHAPTER 22

Perceive to Perform

Once we're out of the Craftsman's office, Faisal and I scurry toward the intercom mic. I don't have much experience with technology, but I see a button, press it, and begin talking.

"Every kid, no matter jinn or human, come to the center of the working quarters!"

Children snap their heads at the sound of my voice, slinking toward us with raised brows. I see other humans, and I wonder when they were tricked into being laborers, and if their qareens were just as obnoxious and sly as mine. Then I see jinn children halt their sweeping of the cement floor, clothes in a stained and ripped state as they wipe sweat off their brows. Tonight, they'll toil away for another day's work. But tomorrow, as long as I'm behind it, they'll be free.

"Most of you have heard the rumors: the Sijj Palace's promise of luxury and patronage is all just a trick. There is no happy ending as long as we're in the working quarters, tied to this hotel."

The children break into whispers, some mentioning Raisal's decline. I notice tiger-toothed Sughal from earlier agreeing with my claims as he explains what happened to other jinn.

"So tonight, we're going to destroy this hotel. No more magic to bind us, no more working for people who exploit us, no more frauds—only truth."

"But...what will we have left?" a quiet jinn girl from the back of the crowd asks me.

I know the human children will be happy with my plan—it allows them to escape the palace and head home. But for jinn children, this is their realm, and for a lot of them, their home *is* the hotel. To them, the owner is just another contractor, just a person they're forced to work under to make ends meet.

But I've heard it from the other jinn—some have debts to pay, others are sold into working. I can eliminate it all if this palace ceases to exist.

"A choice," I say, voice loud and clear. "A choice to work under another selfish employer and do this all over again or to take a chance and seek out a better destiny."

Gasps flicker across the room, but there are snickers too, laughter bursting from the corners. Do they think I'm bluffing? That this is all a joke? I'm about to shout over them, when suddenly the crowd falls silent and parts on its own. And when I see who strides to the front, even I go breathless.

Raisal stands before me, hands balled into fists. He's in the same dingy gray working clothes as the rest of us, all the luxury he enjoyed the day before wiped clean as if with the snap of a finger.

"I'd rather save my own skin than work with humans," he says.

I shake my head. Has he not learned anything from that parlor? You can't escape this vicious cycle by continuing it.

"... is what I thought before I realized the truth," he finishes, swallowing a lump in his throat. "I know a lot of us jinn are hardwired tricksters. It's in our instincts. But we've been fooled. We were only ever tricking ourselves."

The jinn children watch him with quiet gasps, listening intently as he tells his story—of working for so long to become a guest at the hotel, to feel like he mattered, only for Mirza to strip it all away in a moment. The children don't take their eyes off him.

Raisal marches forward and stands next to me. "Let's do this."

Everyone bursts into yells and shouts. There's some disagreement; some furrow their brows in deep thought, while others are already itching to wreak havoc.

"If you want to help, form a line outside the welding room. We're going to bring this palace down."

Faisal and I slip away from the crowd. It's not an easy decision for the jinn to make, so I don't want to bulldoze my plan down their throats. But I notice some twinkling eyes, some small, hopeful smiles. There may not be many of them, but I already see a few groups forming, crowds of kids tailing us as we head toward the welding room.

The stage is set. Long conveyor belts stretch across the chamber, tools and wires placed every meter. The furnaces are burning bright, flames flickering across the walls as if we've stepped into some underworld factory. The window of the welding room slides open and the Craftsman pokes his head out, chiming, "I'm starting it up!"

The floor buzzes as the conveyor belts whirr to life. The kids gasp, eyes wide with excitement as the Craftsman sends out metal after unknown metal.

"Don't worry about the specifics. Everyone just needs

to do their part and follow my lead!" The Craftsman demonstrates how to solder, combining two different wires as if they'd always only been one. Faisal and I grab the tools too, and even if I don't enjoy getting into an assembly line with a bunch of swindling jinn, at least we make a good team.

Is this how a group project works? I've never done science experiments, and I really don't think anyone should trust me with explosives, but it's not all numbers and equations. Us human kids are given simple instructions: put two and two together, as easy as weaving bracelets or slapping brick on brick. Once we've finished our parts, we hand them over to the jinn kids, and that's when things start getting *interesting*.

I pass my tiny contraption to Sughal. He grasps it, squeezes it gently in his hands, and the contraption starts glowing. Fire power. Magic. Whatever these jinn possess is bringing the device to life.

My jaw is still hanging when Sughal passes it to the jinn beside him and asks me for the next part. I clear my throat. Sure, that was cool. Heck, pretty amazing actually. But I'm not a slacker. I twist two bolts into place and hand him the next contraption.

"Hey." Sughal nudges me as he does that weird glowing thing again. "Are we really getting out of here?"

"If you stop talking so much, we'll have a better chance," I grunt.

He bites his lip. "I chose the wrong source of inspiration earlier. You're much more admirable."

My fingers pause in the tangle of wires. His words make my heart lurch. I don't work for glory; everything I do is to survive. Being a top miner because it meant more money, chasing the idea of the Demiurge to escape, and now even building a bomb just so I can see my family again. I try to pull out their smiles from my memories, but my lungs clench. Their faces are blurry. I can't remember what they look like.

Sughal squeezes my shoulder. "Thanks for thinking about us too."

A dry chuckle escapes my lips. What would Maa think now, if she saw me shoulder to shoulder with the heathens in our nightmares? But maybe she'd see me kindling a new hope in their eyes and pat my back, proud. And maybe she'd see how they've lit a fire in me too.

Maybe it's because my memories are blurring and the recent ones are getting the foggiest, but my mind pulls out a memory I'd long forgotten, the voice of someone I haven't seen in years.

"*You'll be more than this,*" Baba says as he ruffles my hair. The ground is sparkling. I think we're near the mica mines. "*There is so, so much more out there. I wish I was able to show you. Become better than me, Nura. Then, one day, you'll not only see it all for yourself but show it to others too.*"

"You okay?" The jinn beside me cocks his head. "Why are you crying?"

❖

Once the Craftsman collects all the separate parts, he locks himself away in the welding room. He said to wait until ten o'clock, but the clock doesn't even hit nine-thirty before the door creaks open. My nose cringes at the fumes. I smack my chest to stop a coughing fit as a figure walks out from the cloud of smoke. The haze clears away, revealing a man covered in grease, with wires poking out every pocket of his stained overalls. The Craftsman lifts his welding mask and under a layer of sweat, there's a smile beaming on his face.

"It's done," he breathes.

His hands tremble from exhaustion as he passes me a tennis-ball-sized bomb. It's heavier than the baskets of dirt I carry out of the tunnels, but I'm glad it's a lot more compact. I can't imagine the look on the jinn's faces if they saw me heaving a giant bomb across the hotel.

The surface shimmers like silk, and when I poke it, colors ripple across like a kaleidoscope. There's magic in here, that's for sure. The hard work of humans and the sprinkle of sorcery from jinn make this a group project to be remembered for centuries. As long as I don't screw up the presentation.

"It's not the exploding kind." He chuckles at my raised brows. "A little dimensional twist here, a sprinkle of magic there...and you have a device both destructive and constructive."

I snicker. "As long as it works."

"You need to find the core of the Space ward; it should be near the casino. When it's eleven p.m., you should hear the giant bell ring. It'll ring again at eleven thirty, and one final time at twelve a.m. When you hear the bell for eleven thirty, that's when I'll stop time for sixty seconds. Plant the bomb, then press this button"—he shows me a fire symbol on the side of it—"and the bomb will turn green. Remember to search for a yellow door before you plant it."

"Because yellow doors are portals to the Matter ward?" Faisal asks.

"Exactly. You'll have sixty seconds before the bomb goes off."

I raise my brows. The Craftsman left a lot out from his speech earlier. I try to give him my most unimpressed scowl, but he just pats my head with his greasy glove.

"I know you can do it. You're the number one mica miner in Meerabagh, aren't you?"

His words shoot straight to my ego. Blood pumps through my veins, injecting me with an intense zap of determination. All I'm thinking of as I meet the sparkling gaze of the Craftsman is *I'll be better, Baba. I'll see it, and I'll show Maa, Adeel, Kinza, and Rabia too. Don't worry.*

"I could do this in my sleep," I humph, slipping the bomb into the pocket of my shalwar.

"Don't forget to gather every single person in the Matter ward. *Every last one,*" the Craftsman says.

"Leave it to us, sir. We have a plan," Faisal replies, grinning.

The Craftsman puts a hand on our shoulders, brows tilted. His red eyes shine not with a bloodthirsty desire like Mirza's or a flaming anger like the owner's—instead, his eyes gleam like the twinkle of stars on an inky night. If we fail, this may be the last time I'll ever see him. It's strange to think that I could feel this way about a jinn, but I'll miss him.

He smiles. "I'll see you on the outside."

CHAPTER 23

Where There's a Will, There's a Way

Faisal and I certainly have a plan. Why we didn't discuss it in front of the Craftsman—well, it's because he might have tried to stop us out of sheer disappointment.

But we're kids without an education. We don't do extensive research or outline schemes and make revisions. We're creatures of guts and intuition—of chaos and mayhem, and that's exactly what we're about to showcase.

As we stroll into the Space ward, there's a crowd of human and jinn children split into different corners of the room. I see Aroofa tightly clutching Sadia's hand, both crouched in the shadows. Tahir's hiding behind a counter, and a bunch of others blend into the surroundings—holding trays of food or offering refreshments. When their gazes snap to me, I snicker. We're all invisible. It's the perfect setup. The party's about to start.

The bright red lights of the Laal Casino are flashing. Patrons chat in bars and line up outside the comedy club. It's ten thirty p.m., peak hours of Sijj Palace festivity. I scan the area more closely, trying to pick out our first victim. That's when I hear the annoyed sneer of a red-dressed woman coming from the comedy club line. She holds a cocktail in one hand, while the other shoves away a nearby man as he tries scooting closer to her. He rests a hand on her shoulder, but she swats it away and growls, "Back off."

"Why don't we settle their squabble, Faisal?" I smirk and crack my knuckles.

"Making things worse i-isn't what I call *settling* a squabble, Nura," he groans.

Before Faisal can slip into another lecture about being careful and taking precautions, I reach into my shalwar for two matchboxes. I hand one to Faisal and pull a match from the other.

"Are you ready to get out of here?" I whisper to him.

"If it m-means I can see my family again, I'm more ready than I've been my entire life."

I pat his shoulder. Faisal heaves a deep breath before

striking his match against the box and slinking over to the comedy club line.

I don't know how well the owner of the Sijj Palace thought it through when he decided to make us children invisible. Even if we are eyesores to the jinn around us, we've been given an unexpected power I'm sure the owner will regret.

I crouch next to the sleazy man, lighting my match. I bring the flame to the hem of his pants, and the threads instantly catch on fire. He yelps, spinning around and pointing a shaking finger at the red-dressed woman.

"What do you think you're doing?" he yells.

The woman rolls her eyes. "Avoiding you. I didn't do anything!"

"You wench," he grumbles. "All I did was ask a few questions and you burn me?"

"You're trying to set me up!" she counters.

Laughter boils in my stomach and seizes my limbs as I burst into a fit of giggles. For jinn, throwing around fire is like playing catch—it doesn't actually burn them, since they're made of it, but it can be quite annoying when they're caught off guard.

I signal with my hands to the other kids, and they continue our plan. Tahir slinks toward another lady and brings his lit match to her studded blue lehnga. Not even three seconds go by before the entire bottom half of her lehnga is engulfed in flames. She screams and stumbles backward.

"It's him!" the first woman yells.

The two female jinn look like they've crept out from the underworld with the scowls that burn on their faces and the glares that seem to freeze anyone they land on. In a fit of rage, balls of fire form in their hands. *Yes. Do it.* I lick my lips when I see our scheme coming together.

I don't plan on destroying the Sijj Palace in one clean explosion. I'm going to burn it piece by piece, letting the owner know that us children are out to get him. That we're about to uncover his dirty history in a night of chaos.

Watch out.

It's what I would've said to Faisal if I'd had enough time, but with the flaming sphere that's heading toward us, I shove Faisal out of the way only a split second before the fire would've torched his hair off. Instead, it hits the sleazy man, and he gasps when the fire singes his shoulder.

Being invisible means we might get caught between the jinn's line of fire. But Faisal and I are quick on our feet, years of mining experience keeping us nimble. Faisal skids over to a group of bearded jinn that sit at the bar counter and lights each of their jackets on fire one by one.

One of them falls off his chair, and the other jumps from his seat and grabs the bartender by the collar. "Hey! What's the meaning of this?" he screeches.

I'm snickering as I tiptoe along the walls, hiding in slivers of shadow, careful so the worker jinn don't see me. The jinn kids join in, summoning balls of fire and launching them across the Space ward like a game of baseball.

I approach the entrance of the Laal Casino, and when I see the crowd at the poker table preoccupied, I sneak closer.

Their brows are furrowed in concentration. Even the dealer is too absorbed with shuffling cards to see my crouched form swoop under the table.

I light another match and drop it right on one jinn's lap.

He shouts as his hands flail and his cards go flying. "Someone burned me! You cheaters." Instantly, he enacts his revenge with fireballs of his own, torching all the cards at the table. The other players spring to their feet, screaming at the unfairness, but not afraid to spray flames of their own.

I roll from under the table and into a corner, watching it all settle into place.

Faisal wheezes as he comes up next to me, throwing the empty matchbox on the floor. "I-it's done," he pants.

I lick my lips. "It is."

All around us, jinn are screaming. They run around in

circles, chasing one another with fireballs in their hands. Flames dance across the luxury carpet and up the walls, reaching the intricately carved wooden chandeliers. Worker jinn run back and forth in an attempt to soothe the mayhem, but every patron's chaos has been completely released.

I'm sweating with how much fire has already engulfed the Space ward. And then I hear it: the last step in the first stage of our plan.

"This is an emergency signal. Everyone, please make your way to the Matter ward in a calm manner."

The Craftsman told me this would happen. As the speakers across the Space ward ring with that message, jinn screech and shove to reach the exit. I glue myself to the wall as a horde of jinn empty out of the Laal Casino. Smoke clogs the air in a gray haze, and I crouch low to give my lungs a break. Fire starts to paint the walls black, and the signs and bulbs of the Laal Casino burst and topple to the ground in an eruption of sparks.

A train of flames approaches the entrance of the casino. Faisal yelps as he jumps out of the way, but now he's on the outside and I'm on the inside, and there's a wall of fire taller than the both of us in between.

"Nura," he yells.

"I'm okay," I say. I can still see his wide eyes through the flicker of flames. "Our plan worked."

"But the bomb—"

"I'll go search for the core of the Space ward and plant it. Go make sure everyone's made it into the Matter ward. Don't forget the other worker kids."

Faisal steps a little closer to the flames. I can hear how loudly he swallows a lump in his throat. "Nura, be careful in there. You could pass out from the smoke. And the lights are going out, it'll be d-dark soon...."

There's a nerve in my brain that snaps at the thought of listening to another one of Faisal's cautionary rants, but I clench my hands into fists. What if our plan doesn't work, and this is the last time I'll hear it? What if this is the last time Faisal will ever warn me? Even if my lungs feel like combusting, I let him release every word he's straining to say. If he comes out of this alive and I don't, he'll feel so overwhelmingly guilty about not offering every last bit of caution that I'm sure he'll blame himself for it.

I smile to him from across the flames, and as they flicker, I see him smile back.

"Nura," he says, voice so quiet I barely hear him over the crackle of fire and the crash of chandeliers.

"Yeah?"

"When we get to Mr. Waleed's cart, I'll buy you gulab jamun."

I snort. "You said your family's saving every rupee. It's fine—"

"I never buy sweets because I never have a reason to. But now I do."

I can't tell if it's because of the fire in front of me, but my cheeks feel incredibly hot. "You're hopeless—"

"Thanks for coming to save me, Nura."

He really is hopeless. Not just because he considered that I might *not* come for him, but because he doesn't realize that I know he'd do the same for me too. Whether it's because he wants to avoid a lecture from his maa, or the mines have collapsed, or we're stuck in a hotel for jinn, I'll save him each and every time.

CHAPTER 24

The Fool and the Trickster

The smoke is so thick I could lie beneath it like a blanket. My lungs are begging me for fresh air, but I keep my breaths as shallow as I can, tucking my chin under my kameez as I scour the ravaged Laal Casino.

Faisal, the employees, and the patrons have left me alone in the Space ward. But even as I peer across the walls and turn over slot machines, I can't seem to find any hint of its core. All the Craftsman told me is that it's somewhere around the Laal Casino. He may be a legendary architect known to all as the Demiurge, but he's *horrible* at giving directions.

Where could it be? I don't have much time to think before I'll be roasted like a slab of goat meat. I stop crawling across the scruffy carpet to review what I know. What would the *core* be? Is it a place? An object? The heart of the hotel?

I wipe the sweat from my upper lip. What could be at the heart of the hotel? At the heart of the owner who controls it?

My eyes widen.

The Craftsman had been telling us the entire time. *He threw away his morals for money. He deserted me for money.* I scoff. I should've realized it sooner. Money—that's the core of this hotel. That's what tore apart the two brothers who created the Sijj Palace, and it's why I'll destroy it.

I look to my left and see one of the only signs still flashing: THE VAULTS.

The vaults—where all the cash reserves of the casino would be stored away in safes. My fingers tingle. This is it.

I stumble over to the giant windows at the side of the casino that overlook the brilliant sea below. The sky is a deep purple, and far below, pink waves coast calmly to shore. I grab a fallen lantern from the ground and throw it against the window. The glass shatters, and the broken hole is big enough for smoke to escape.

Now that the smoke will clear up, I head toward the door leading to the vaults. I grab the handle and open it. My heart drops.

It's pitch-black.

Fire illuminates a meter in front of me, but I can't see anything beyond. The electricity has probably gone out, so I don't bother looking for a light switch. Instead, I snatch a candle pot off the ground, swipe it in the fire, and let its small flame guide me.

This is nothing. I'm Nura, the best mica miner in all of Meerabagh. I've traversed deeper tunnels than whatever lies in store, and I've pranced through darkness more times than I can count. Even if I can barely see, I can still *feel* my way through. *It's the mines all over again*, I tell myself. *You're the best person for the job.*

One of my hands holds the candle pot steady while the other grazes the sides of the walls. I let my touch lead the way, feeling for any temperature drop or hole in the wall that could give me some kind of direction.

My feet splash in small puddles of water, and droplets tap-dance across my head.

"Closer."

I snap my head to the left and follow the voice. It's oddly familiar.

"Come closer."

The hairs on my arm stand on their ends when I realize it's the same raspy voice I heard in the mines the day it collapsed. I run faster until I'm panting. I'm tripping over scuffs in the floor and tumbling against the walls, but I *know* this is the right way. It may just be the instinct of a miner, or the tug of magic, but I feel the pull.

"Gah!"

I stumble back as my nose crashes into something. The candle pot drops to the floor, flames sprinting along the walls and lighting up any stray twigs and paper. The tunnels illuminate—displaying stony walls with a curved ceiling, and right in front of me, a smirk on her face, is my qareen.

"You're supposed to be slaving away in the working quarters. What do you think you're doing here?" she rumbles.

I get to my feet, dusting off my trousers. Dura may think she has the upper hand just because she's a jinn and this is her realm, but I'm in my element. I'm not scared of her like I was the first day we met. Everything overwhelmed me then—the strange colors of this world, the monstrous appearance of the jinn, the endless luxury. She was clever to flaunt my greatest weakness and show me things I never even *imagined* I could want. But she is my qareen—cunning is our middle name.

Except I'm no longer that greedy girl who first stepped into the Sijj Palace and couldn't keep her jaw from hanging.

"I don't have time for petty tricks, Dura."

"Then I'll make this simple for you."

She lunges at me, pointy fingers like daggers. I dodge at the last second, rolling to the side.

"You'll never be happy in the human realm," Dura growls. "All you'll ever be is surrounded by dirt."

She launches her foot in a kick, but I block with my arm and hop aside again.

"Aren't I doing the same thing here?" I counter. "You want me to work for an eternity in this hotel just so you won't have to. But you saw Raisal. There isn't hope here for any of us."

Shadows dance over Dura's grim face as the flames flicker. "Raisal was an idiot to anger the Painted Boy. I won't make the same mistake."

I release a shaky breath. Why is she purposely turning a blind eye? "It's not about *mistakes*. Mistakes are just excuses. They would've done this to us anyway."

Dura grits her teeth. "I used to have everything, and if you're going to stand in the way of me gaining it all back, don't think I won't try to stop you."

I don't have to stick around to find out how. A ball of fire forms in her hands, and she launches it like a rock toward me. I sprint down the tunnels, heart galloping, sweat dripping into my eyes.

But every single limb in my body jolts when I hear the first ring of the giant bell in the distance. *It's eleven p.m.*

I need to get to the center of the vaults and plant the bomb within half an hour, or the Craftsman's work will be useless. I can't activate the bomb if he doesn't stop time in the Matter ward, because that would mean everyone would go down *with* the Sijj Palace.

Flames lick my hair, and the rancid stench of burning stings my nose. Dura is catching up to me, her raspy laughter echoing off the stony walls. She flings more fire my way. My movements are lagging now, legs begging me to stop.

I'm used to overworking, used to digging deeper and harder than the other kids. But I can't compete with a jinn—they're so much stronger, so much faster than I can ever be. With every spurt of speed, I'm losing more energy, but Dura only seems to be enjoying our chase more.

I groan as I run faster. I'm not going to give up—I have to make it back to my family and help out Maa. Maa works twice, no, five times harder than I do. She gives up her bowl of rice to Kinza and Rabia, and still decides to tell Adeel a bedtime story when she should be sleeping to prepare for an early day of work. And I know that no matter how many times she begs me to quit mining—it's because she can't bear to lose another one of her loved ones to it.

I wish I could hear her now, even if it's just another one

of her shouting lectures where she chases me around the house with a wooden spoon. I wish she could sing me a song, or read me the Quran, or tell me a story.

I gasp.

The memory comes in flashes and spurts; I've lost too much of it for it to be whole, but I remember the last story Maa told me.

Your baba recited Ayat al-Kursi. It's the throne verse in the Quran. God will always protect you from harm if you recite it.

I know that verse by heart. Maa always recites it before sleep, blowing kisses onto our foreheads when she finishes. She's done it every day for years.

I spin around. Dura's morbid smile flashes in the low light. Her claws are stretched toward my throat, and her fangs glisten in the firelight. Even though I see myself in her, she's the worst monster of my nightmares.

"Allah, there is no divine being except him, he is the creator of all existence," I say in Arabic.

Dura slows, her feet jerking to a stop.

"He never tires, and whatever lies in the heavens and on earth, all belongs to him."

Dura's eyes widen. I swallow, clearing my throat and speaking louder.

"Who can intercede with him unless he permits? He knows

the past, the present, and what comes after, and no one will encompass what he does not will."

"What are you doing?" Dura shrieks. Her mouth is curled in a wild snarl, but she doesn't come closer. She *can't*.

"His throne extends over the heavens and earth, and watching over their preservation tires him not, for he is the highest and greatest being."

As I finish the verse, Dura drops to her knees. She peers up at me, but there's no fury or amusement in her eyes. Just astonishment.

I sigh. My body feels lighter—as if I've dropped a heavy weight from my shoulders. There's not even an ounce of fear within me anymore. I feel invincible—watched over by the angels, cradled in God's arms. I step closer to Dura and curl my hand around hers.

"Head to the Matter ward, and don't stir up too much trouble when I'm gone. You'll tarnish our name."

And then I turn and dash down the tunnels, grinning as the door of the vaults comes into view.

CHAPTER 25

All Thoughts Must Be Mortal

The Craftsman warned me.

As I stand inside the vaults that look like an ancient cistern, with a high arched ceiling and polished granite floor, I'm face-to-face with the owner of the Sijj Palace.

Bubbles of magma hiss from his mouth, and his eye sockets burn with dancing flames. He stands at the center of the circular room, chambers of different vaults surrounding us. I glance around, gaze skipping across the room until it lands on a bright yellow door. *A portal to the Matter ward.* My ticket out of here. But it's right behind the owner. He must've known I was coming.

"I'm not going to let you burn down these vaults," he growls.

Oh, I have a lot worse planned for this place.

I'm waiting for the bell to ring eleven thirty. It could be any minute now. But until then, I have to keep myself from getting melted by the owner. I need to buy some time.

"Why'd you do it?" I yell.

"Enslave children to work for the hotel?" he jests. "It's not like you were going to become anything in the human realm. Children like you are just flecks of dirt. No one will care that you're gone."

A few weeks ago, I might've agreed with him. Whenever I dug in the mines, I never left with any mica in my pockets—just a thick layer of dirt caked on my skin. I was working for someone else, someone who probably didn't even know that children were being illegally hired to carve out minerals from the ground. I was a nobody.

But I'd rather be a nobody with a family I love than somebody who abandons their own.

"I mean, why'd you desert your brother? Why did you lock the Demiurge away in the working quarters?"

The owner's shoulders slump, as if I've spilled a secret he knew was coming back to bite him. "My brother knows nothing about business. If I'd left the hotel in his hands, do you think it would've been such a success? Brought in all the money it has? I had to do it." He clutches his chest, coughing. It's only then that I notice the cracks in his charred, rocky skin, and the lava pouring from it like blood.

"Your soul is tied to this palace just like the Craftsman's, isn't it?" Wires start clicking in my brain. Switches turn on. If they both created the Sijj Palace, then both their souls are tied to this hotel. "The Space ward is burning down. You're using up all your magic to keep it standing, aren't you?"

The owner huffs and reaches out a hand to support himself against the wall. The Craftsman can probably feel the ward collapsing in a sea of fire, but he's not going to do anything about it. The owner's a different case—the Sijj Palace is his entire livelihood, his pride, the only thing keeping all his self-hatred contained.

"I'm not here to burn down the vaults, *sir*," I say as if I've ever learned proper manners in my life. "I'm here to plant this."

I slip the bomb out of my pocket. The owner gasps, leaning his entire body against a vault door. Magma no longer flows under his burnt skin, it's all just cooling rock now. I finally see his eyes for the first time, without the flames lighting them up. They're just a dark pair of wide, scared eyes. I wonder if this is how he looked all those years ago when people doubted him—so afraid of a penniless future that he sank low enough to exploit children.

"Don't. I'll give you anything. You won't have to work anymore!" he wheezes. "You can stay a patron forever."

I scoff. It's like Mirza's marriage proposal, without all the strings attached. *Tempting.* I could have VIP status like Shahmaran, who's offered platters of delicacies at her every beck and call. Or I could be like Mirza, an icon, a princess to the other patrons who admire my every step and glance.

It's everything I could want and more. It's the perfect dream.

But then I remember the beautiful illusion in the working quarters, the room painted with the night sky and glittering like a canvas of constellations. The Craftsman's voice echoes in my head.

Those that are and those that become... These are the only two possibilities. And in our world, you shouldn't hope for anything more than a likely story.

A smirk snaps onto my face. Perfection doesn't exist. The idea of the owner's offer sounds incredible—I could live my life drowning in a bed of cushions with a syrupy gulab on my tongue. I almost sigh at the thought of it. But the real world isn't one to grant such impossible fantasies. This trip to the Sijj Palace has already taught me that.

When I try to imagine such a life... I can't help but cringe. What would I do with it all? What's the point of wanting things just for the sake of wanting them? I'm not that person anymore.

The bell rings in the distance.

I don't know if Faisal gathered every single person in the Matter ward. I don't even know if the Craftsman was able to stop time at this very moment. But I trust them. I trust them more than anything the owner can offer me.

"History repeats itself." I sigh, settling the bomb at the center of the room. "Once again, we fall to chaos."

"Please, don't..."

I click the fire button on the side of the bomb. It transforms into a ball of green light, glowing brighter with each second.

"You—" the owner gasps.

"But we'll rise again. And again. And once more."

There are still many criminals like the hotel owner out there—and there won't stop being people like him in the future either. Places like this will be replaced, recreated, but right now, it's just me, the hotel owner, and a crumbling Sijj Palace. All I care about is ending his reign of trickery.

The bomb's light turns the entire vaults into a pool of green. Twenty seconds remain. I sprint toward the yellow door, but before I grasp the knob to open it, my gaze drops to the haggard owner.

He's practically just stone now, hard and brittle, frozen as time ticks away. I could leave him here. He deserves it for enslaving all those children. But the Craftsman told Faisal and me to gather *every single person* into the Matter ward. If Faisal has everyone else, then I can manage one person. I don't do it for the owner, or for my own conscience. I do it for the Craftsman—the only jinn I'd call a friend.

CHAPTER 26

One and Continuous

When I grabbed the owner's arm and dashed through the yellow door, I didn't expect to be met with a whirlwind of madness.

In a split second I see everything and nothing—the world and all it encompasses, the dark space around it in all its uncharted glory. Shouts and yelps echo in my ears. Wind rips across my limbs like I've been sucked into a tempest.

It feels like eternity and just one second. It feels like life.

When my eyes stutter open, there's a pale-purple sky above me. A horde of strange birds fly in circles, chirping. Crimson clouds drift by. My brain feels like a pile of mud, and every nerve in my body jerks awake as if I've been struck by lightning. I look around me.

Destruction.

I'm sitting on a pile of stones, wood, and tiles. All around me are other confused faces, jinn and human children, their eyes wide as they look across the ocean of the Sijj Palace debris.

We did it. I spring to my feet, bursting into laughter as I jump high in the air. I pump my fist skyward, stumbling on rocks and battered wooden boards, but I couldn't care less. I taste fresh air for the first time in what feels like weeks. The breeze tickles my cheeks like a caress. I'm tempted to throw off my sandals and run down to the shore so I can plant my feet in the soil.

I notice Raisal's scruffy hair sticking out at wild angles from across the wreckage. He's limping, another jinn's arm slung across his shoulders, and I can't help the small smile that melts onto my face. He's carrying Dura with him, both of them finding a warm spot under the sun. All of a sudden I remember the mines again, the day they collapsed, and the way Faisal pulled me out because he knew to never leave a friend behind.

Then to my right, dancing over a pile of ripped curtains, I see Aroofa twirling Sadia in the air, their giggles bouncing across the breeze. "Baji!" Sadia squeals as she jumps into Aroofa's arms. Tahir sits beside them, clapping his hands to the beat of their spinning.

I see other human children, those who didn't work in the mines, look to the sky as if they're staring at a breathtaking painting. How long they must've been stuck in the hotel is beyond me, but from the way their knees tremble from the weight of all the world is now offering them, I know it must've been decades. Will they find a way back home? Or perhaps, have they grown so accustomed to this realm that the thought of leaving doesn't interest them?

The girl with the Punjabi accent I met back in the working quarters is staring at the sea with wide eyes, fingers twitching. A grin blooms onto her face as she jumps into the air. "I remember now! I lived near the Ravi River."

Even my own memories are rushing back to me. The sound of Kinza's and Rabia's giggles. The bright green of Maa's dupatta. The earthy smell of well-trodden soil as I walked to and from the mica mines.

And then I look to my left.

His hair is unwound, cascading across his shoulders like waves of the clearest blue ocean, red eyes twinkling as he gazes up at the sky. His lips are parted like he can't believe it all.

"Craftsman!" I yell.

He jolts out of his trance and whips his head to me. That's when I see it—the brightest smile in the world. It could rival the sun. Outshine the largest bonfire. Dazzle more brilliantly than the North Star.

"Nura," he says. "We're free."

I've never seen anyone look so happy to see their own creation destroyed, but the Craftsman is glowing.

"We are." I smile.

Arms wrap around me from behind, and I yelp in surprise. Curly dark hair wisps onto my cheek, and I spin around to complete the hug. "Faisal!"

"We did it." He gasps. "I c-can't believe we did it."

The Craftsman joins in and pulls us both into a hug. "It's been a while since you two have been home, hasn't it? You should get going before your families turn ill from worrying. Try not to miss the jinn realm too much."

I laugh and smack the Craftsman's arm. "What about you? What are you going to do now that you're free?"

The Craftsman's gaze lingers over the wreckage of the Sijj Palace, the debris filling probably an entire kilometer. He smiles as he watches the children, human and jinn alike, jumping in joy as they slide down floorboards and toss casino tokens in a game of catch.

"I think I'll build a school," he says.

Faisal's eyes light up. "A—a school?"

The Craftsman nods. "I've been thinking.... If we'll fall to chaos again in an inevitable cycle, then why not try to make the world last as long as possible before that happens? Educating people, eliminating their ignorance...I believe that's the best way to keep chaos in check."

I smile. Perhaps it is. "I wish I could stick around to enroll."

I don't feel the same dislike for school that I used to. Now it seems interesting—exciting, even—to battle the chaos inside me and come out enlightened. Except my family's waiting for me. I can't stay here forever.

"I wish you could too." The Craftsman sighs. "But I can offer you something else. I would only pass it down to a very special person."

I spring forward. "What is it?"

Faisal groans, raising a brow. "What happened to not being greedy?"

The Craftsman laughs. "My human counterpart visited the Sijj Palace once, many years ago. I gave him a present as we bid our goodbyes. But he never came back."

The Craftsman raises his chin to the sky, embracing the cool breeze as it flutters his suit and whisks his blue hair into a dance. "I don't think he'll be needing that present anymore. It got lost. But I know where you can find it."

"Where?" I gasp. I'm practically electrified with anticipation.

The Craftsman pulls out a slip of paper and a pen from his suit. My mouth hangs open when he draws a rough map of Meerabagh. He must've come to spend time with his human counterpart often. Then he strikes a certain spot with an X and hands the paper to me.

"This might be your last mission as the best mica miner in Meerabagh. Go find it. I, on the other hand, have one very broken person to mend."

The Craftsman's gaze skims over debris until it lands on a soot-stained, flaky man, cradled against a smashed slot machine. I narrow my eyes, but I still can't believe it—it's the owner, reduced to a pile of burnt charcoal, refusing to lift his head and face reality.

"You don't have to...," I mutter. "He isn't worth more than dirt."

The Craftsman smiles, closing his eyes as he inhales a gulp of salty, fresh air. "But sometimes"—he sighs, ruffling my hair—"if you dig hard enough, you can find sparkles in the dirt, can't you?"

I break into a grin. Grabbing Faisal with one hand and the Craftsman with the other, I pull them in to share one more hug.

CHAPTER 27

Dirt in the Sparkles

When Faisal and I pop our heads out from the mica mines, it's dawn. The dark sky is glittering with an underbelly of yellow, and I can see the sun peek out from above the horizon, welcoming us home.

Faisal cheers, throwing his hands in the air as he flops onto the ground with a sigh. I slump down into a squat next to him, equally exhausted. The mining site looks the same, tape markers outlining the area, holes that you could fall into with just a single misstep, and piles upon piles of sparkling dirt.

I've never been so happy to be here.

We sit there for a while, chests heaving, blood still

rushing through our veins. The dark sky cracks open, and dawn trickles in. Shy yellow light flickers over the mines, painting its hills golden, every inch and angle twinkling. My breath hitches. Faisal's frozen too. It's always been here, but I've never stopped to just steep in its beauty. Magic isn't only reserved for the jinn realm; it's here too if we look long enough.

"It's starting again," I breathe. "A clean slate."

I slip the Craftsman's map out of my pocket. My eyes narrow in the dim light, trying to identify every single marker the Craftsman sketched.

"Hey, Faisal..." I sit up, scanning the area. I shove the map in his face, and he groans, swatting it away.

"Can't we search for the present later? I think I'm g-gonna take a nap here."

I smack the top of his head. "Look. Doesn't the X point to the mines?"

He jerks upright at that, snatching the piece of paper. His gaze flickers across the map like a metronome, and instantly he jumps to his feet.

"Nura, grab your shovel."

I lick my lips. I seize the nearest shovel and follow Faisal to the east of the mining site, heading into abandoned mining territory. These are old tunnels where all the mica's been extracted and there's little reason to keep digging.

But now I have a different reason.

Faisal paces back and forth as he bites his lips. He glances at the sun, then back down, then at the radio tower in the distance. When he licks a finger to test for the wind's direction, I'm about to pounce on him and tell him to stop playing games, but he beats me to it.

"Here. Dig here."

I strike my shovel against the dirt. The ground crumbles away immediately, and I fall into a shallow hole. I still don't see anything. "You better not be testing me so early in the morning, Faisal. I'm grouchy when I don't get enough sleep."

"I assure you, my b-brain is still working."

So I dig for another ten minutes, but all I see is dirt. Faisal joins in, and we expand the hole, Faisal digging to the east and me to the west. We continue until our backs are soaked in sweat, minutes upon minutes passing by. It isn't until the sun has practically risen that my shovel clangs against something hard.

"Over here, Faisal!"

We dig around the object, striking away dirt bit by bit. I raise my brows when I see a purple box the size of a book, made of shimmering metal that changes colors with every glance. I blow the dust off it and pinch the clamp until the box springs open.

Faisal gasps. My heart freezes.

Inside the box, shining as if it was made just yesterday, is a large golden key. It's dense and heavy when I lift it. Gems of every color and cut are embedded in the handle, and I inhale sharply when I see small flecks of clear stone that glitter like a rainbow—diamonds.

"H-how?" Faisal stammers, raking a hand through his curls. His brows shoot up to the edge of his forehead.

It's worth a fortune. It has to be priceless—and when I see the small note attached to it, I know I'm right.

Come back in a few years to see its complete greatness. I'll be waiting for you to open the door.

It's the Craftsman's neat scrawl. His present to his human counterpart was a key to the Sijj Palace. I release an amused huff. It's not much use now. The Sijj Palace is destroyed. But I have an inkling as to what I can do with it.

"Faisal?"

"Is that Nura?"

My head snaps upward when I hear shouts.

We glance at each other and then hop out of the hole. I narrow my eyes against the bright yellow of the sunrise, trying to make out who the yelling silhouettes are. But when I realize it's now the middle of the morning, I let out a laugh. It's all the mining children, ready for another day of work.

"You're back? We thought you were dead!"

The kids yell and scream, shoving Faisal and me back and forth to determine if we're ghosts. Ahmed's here too, eyes wide as he pokes my arm, and gasping when he realizes it is, in fact, a perfectly fine me.

And then lo and behold, Aroofa, Sadia, and Tahir are grunting as they climb out of the mines as well. They must've gotten lost somewhere along the way.

But then I hear more shouting, and it isn't the excited yells of kids this time. The brute, rough voices of the contractors echo from the outskirts of the mining site.

"You can't just come here every day. I'm sorry, but it's prohibited."

"I don't care if it's prohibited!" a high, shaky voice screams. "I know my daughter is here somewhere."

When clouds of dust clear and I get a better view of the argument, I see the hunched form of a middle-aged woman, green dupatta wrapped loosely around her head, hands shaking without anything to hold on to.

"Maa!" I yell.

I only see Maa's sobbing face for a split second before she's running toward me and squeezing me into a hug. "Subhanallah," she cries, thanking God for once again being amazing. "I came to the mines every day looking for you. But you're here, you're really here."

Faisal's maa comes running to join the reunion as well, and she envelops him in an equally bone-crushing hug.

Maa pulls back to grab my face in her calloused hands. I've missed her touch. It doesn't feel like the burn of jinn; it feels like the warmth of a human. I grab the front of her kameez and sink my face into her chest.

"How's Adeel? Kinza and Rabia?" I ask, trying not to let my voice tremble. If it does, my mother doesn't comment on it.

"They miss you so much," Maa says, a new stream of tears flowing down her cheeks. I reach up to swipe them away, stretching my lips into the brightest smile I can muster.

"You're never going to mine mica again," she sniffles, kissing my cheeks. "I don't care if I need to work day and night."

"I agree, Maa, I won't mine mica ever again. I have a different plan."

She strokes my head, already back into the routine of indulging in my little games. But this time, I'm not bluffing.

I pull out the priceless key to the Sijj Palace. *The Demon's Tongue*. Sunlight shines off it like a wink.

"We can sell this and build a school. One big enough that none of these kids will ever have to mine mica again."

The Craftsman was right. This really was my last mission as Meerabagh's best mica miner.

Faisal escapes his mother's clutch to place a hand on my shoulder. His lips coil into a smile of wonder, joy, and most of all, hope for what comes next. It mirrors the expression on all the kids around me—a gaze that sparkles not from the immediate satisfaction of food and money...but the realization that they can dream for something bigger.

"Do you trust me?" I whisper.

He chuckles. "More than myself."

AUTHOR'S NOTE

For some kids, fear is seeing jinn at night; it's that unsettling realm of tricks and traps, it's the nightmares we think of when reality doesn't quite match up with our imagination. Yet, for a lot of kids, fear *is* their reality. Kids like Nura and Faisal exist today, all over the world, thrown into forced labor to make ends meet.

The sparkling dirt mentioned in this book, mica, is a real mineral, mined globally in places like India, Madagascar, and Brazil. In many cases, the method of excavating the mineral is illegal and deadly, and more often than not the workers hired for the job are children—some as young as five years old. Not only is there the risk of the mines collapsing, but inhaling the dangerous underground gases can lead to numerous illnesses, like tuberculosis and silicosis. And not to mention broken bones, exhaustion, and heat stroke.

Physical harm is only one danger that threatens these

children. There are other risks: violence, abuse, and exploitation. As children are sent away from home, separated from their caregiver, and put under the supervision of employers who may not mean well—power imbalances form, and this places them in very vulnerable situations.

As I'm writing this, there are an estimated 160 million children victim to child labor worldwide, and almost half this number are kids aged between five and eleven...kids younger than Nura. The factors that produce child labor are complicated; it's not as easy as asking parents to stop sending their child to work. There's a vicious cycle that's trapped a specific type of family—families that are poor, victims to natural disasters, or suffering through war.

The sad reality is that child labor is preventable. But because of the demand for cheap goods and labor, we as consumers don't even second-guess where many of the products we buy come from, and from what *process*. The makeup one wears? The new paint job on a car? Children are dying for something we wipe off our faces by night, for small satisfactions that don't last.

When I began writing *Nura and the Immortal Palace*, I hadn't known I would end up with a story that pushed for the importance of education. The words flowed so naturally from me I didn't question why or how. I realize now that the theme of education arose because it was ingrained in my own life—my parents and their childhood, and how much they championed school as they raised me. My dad always likes to say, "I got to where I am now because of education. And you started where I ended. Can you imagine, then, how much higher you can reach?"

My dad used to live in a small village in Pakistan, in a one-room house he shared with six other family members. His dad, my grandfather, worked in a tannery, exposed to toxic fumes and strenuous labor. When he came home, he barely spoke, too exhausted to do much else other than eat dinner and fall asleep for another early day of work. Seeing the sick state my grandfather constantly lived in and the horrific conditions of his workplace, my dad realized he didn't want that life for himself, and the only way he could prevent it was through studying his way out.

It was through education that my dad won scholarships to the best engineering programs in the country, the reason he was able to immigrate to Canada, and why he's preached from the second I started kindergarten that school wasn't just a requirement, it was a privilege, and if I regarded it as not just a phase of life but as a *life changer*, then I too could go places—places my dad couldn't reach because he'd started too low on this phenomenon called life.

Education as a means of escape—from poverty, from war, from discrimination—can combat that fearful reality, the terror of thinking your situation can't get any better. If you have one foot already through the door, then it's only a matter of working harder to dig your reality out of the dirt and into a pool of sparkles.

ACKNOWLEDGMENTS

Getting a book published used to be my little secret whispered into wondrous air, hoping I could breathe life into a dream I've envisioned since day one. At first, it was a long, lonely road, but there have been so many people who've joined in on my journey and made it that much more memorable and amazing.

To my tireless, brilliant agent who became my first advocate, thank you so much, Melanie. I was in a tough period of my life and so, *so* close to giving up before you took a chance and decided I was a gem worth polishing. I'll always be grateful for how well you listen, your astute advice, your ability to deeply understand my stories, and your ambition that allows me to push harder and dream bigger. I wish the world had more humans like you.

My editor duo, Ruqayyah Daud and Gráinne Clear, the best tag team I could ask for, I don't think there's enough words to describe what an amazing experience it's been to work alongside you both. Ruqayyah, I'm so grateful for you embracing my book wholeheartedly, understanding the story, world, and characters. Gráinne, you've been an invaluable help, and I can always feel your passion through our calls and emails. Having the two of you advocate for and edit my book has made this experience all the more special. Sometimes it even felt like we were conversing over tea in the margins.

To Caitlyn Averett, I'll never forget our short time together. Our brainstorming calls are still some of the most fun moments I've had. I can't thank you enough for believing in this story and acquiring it as quickly as you did. You're an amazing support, and any author would be lucky to have you.

I can't forget the teams that made this all possible. To the amazing, strong women at Root Literary, you all inspire me every day. To the Little, Brown family, Marisa Finkelstein, Ana Deboo, Virginia Lawther, Sarah Vostok, Bill Grace, Andie Divelbiss, Mara Brashem, Sydney Tillman, Christie Michel, Shawn Foster, Danielle Cantarella, and the rest of the Little, Brown Books for Young Readers team who helped shape this story into book form and got it out into the world, I'm inexplicably grateful.

To T.S. Ferguson, Laura Schreiber, and the rest of the JIMMY team that made the acquisition possible, thank you for giving me a moment I'll never forget.

To Tracy Shaw and Maia Fjord, thank you for making both versions of my book into the beautiful pieces of art it is today. And to my brilliant cover artists, Khadijah Khatib and Hazem Asif, there's magic in your illustrations, and I'm forever grateful for you both sprinkling that charm into this book.

Thanks must also be sent across the world to my UK advocates, the fabulous team at Walker Books, for working wonders on this story.

To Fiona, thank you for cheering me on when I wasn't sure of this book. Your support allowed me to take that dive.

To my parents, who helped check for authenticity and whose eyes sparkled when reading all the nods to our culture, thanks for being there for me. And to my brown girl squad, all the desis I know, thank you for keeping our culture alive even halfway across the world.

And my deepest appreciation to you, my readers.